Could she work for this man? Did she even want to?

Laura looked at a photo on the file cabinet. "I assume this is her?"

Gregory handed it over. "Yes. Taken just before she had Caleb."

A young woman smiled back at her. Love shone in her eyes, giving her a look of radiance and happiness. Was it the loss of her that made Gregory such a quiet, reflective person?

"Very nice." Laura noticed school photos of both sons. Joel definitely had his father's good looks, the same brooding eyes. "I'd be happy to give Caleb lessons if he can work it in between his baseball practice and school homework."

"He will. Caleb can do anything he sets his mind to."

"And Joel?"

"Quite the opposite. He could do it, but he doesn't have the confidence to try."

"Perhaps he needs to be encouraged."

His eyes narrowed. "And you think I don't encourage him?"

"I didn't say that."

"You didn't need to." Gregory leaned over and picked up Caleb's photo, as if to change the subject. "Caleb's like his mother in many ways. He would very much like for me to find a mother for him, but, to be perfectly honest, I have no desire to marry again. Just thought you'd want to know that."

Laura's cheeks flushed for the second time that morning. "Well, I suppose it would be good to let you know I have no intention of marrying again, either. There is no one that could possibly replace my husband, Jerry."

She stood and moved toward the door. Gregory stood also. "Look, I didn't mean to—"

Laura laughed, but it sounded hollow.

BIRDIE L. ETCHISON lives in Washington State and knows much about the Pacific Northwest, the setting for the majority of her books. She loves to research the colorful history of the United States and uses her research along with family stories to create wonderful novels.

Books by Birdie L. Etchison

HEARTSONG PRESENTS
HP123—The Heart Has Its Reasons
HP168—Love Shall Come Again
HP208—Love's Tender Path
HP252—Anna's Hope
HP272—Albert's Destiny

A Tender Melody

Birdie L. Etchison

Heartsong Presents

For my sister, Barbara,
Elsie for editing help,
Evelyn for encouragement,
and Keithanne who lives in beautiful Joseph, Oregon

A note from the author:
I love to hear from my readers! You may correspond with me by writing: **Birdie L. Etchison**
Author Relations
PO Box 719
Uhrichsville, OH 44683

Scripture taken from the HOLY BIBLE INTERNATIONAL VERSION®. NIV®. Copyright© 1973, 1978, 1984 by International Bible Society. Used by permission of Zondervan Publishing House.

ISBN 1-57748-551-3

A TENDER MELODY

Cover illustration by Jocelyne Bouchard.

PRINTED IN THE U.S.A.

one

"It takes a good four years to get over a loss, whether it's from death or divorce."

Pastor Dave's words rang through Laura Madison's mind as she dug holes for the dahlias. He was wrong. It took a lot longer than four years to get over the loss of a beloved husband.

She dug another hole and pushed a tuber into it. She loved flowers and liked having the front yard a riot of colors all year from tulips in the spring, to gladiolas in summer, to dahlias in the fall. Jerry had always been the gardener; consequently, Laura had never spaded the ground, weeded, or even cut the grass until his death. Even now she relied on the help of Renee, her neighbor, who had shown her the best way to dig up the dirt and work compost in. She finished tapping down the earth over the last dahlia tuber when Renee hollered from her porch.

"How about taking a breather? I just put on a pot of tea and have lemon scones hot out of the oven."

Laura straightened and rubbed at a kink in her back. So far her forties had been the pits. This nagging ache in her lower back was noticeable after anything physical such as vacuuming, spading dirt, or hauling bags of groceries from the car.

"Sounds great," she shouted back to Renee. "Let me wash up and get into some clean pants."

The phone was ringing when she entered the house. She removed her dirt clogs first, then her gloves, as she hurried to catch it. She'd been hoping for, yet not quite expecting, a call from northeastern Oregon. The recorder clicked on just as she reached for the phone. A deep, bass voice filled the room.

"This is Reverend Gregory Hall with a message for Laura Madison. I'm responding to the ad placed in the *Chieftain,* our weekly paper. I'd like to discuss the possibility of a position as the pianist in our small community church."

Laura's heart quickened as she started to pick up the receiver to announce she was really there, but something stopped her. She couldn't talk yet.

It had taken weeks of just thinking about it before she found the courage to send for newspapers. She'd then read the "Help Wanted" ads, looking for a position she could fill, knowing she didn't want to be a nanny, sell real estate, or clean motel rooms. A few days later, she'd placed two ads. Now came the next steps: answering the call and going for an interview. Was she up to it? Did she really want to go to the mountains, leave her home in Sealand just three blocks from the Pacific Ocean? What had gotten into her anyway?

She had doubts about this decision, enough so that she hadn't told anyone about her plans to move on. Not even Renee. Especially not Renee.

Laura loved the beach and her community, but every time she passed the fishing docks the memories flooded back. She couldn't bear it any longer. Even with the prayer and support of friends, each day that she strolled the beach, each time she sniffed the salt air, each time she heard a siren or a Coast Guard helicopter, she froze. *Jerry.*

❧

How he'd loved the sea—loved being a commercial fisherman. Always in the back of her mind had been the fear that someday a storm would blow in. . .someday he might not return home.

Then the day came. The knock on her door. Sheriff Dan Olsen stood there, a serious look on his face. "Laura. . ."

She trembled as she motioned him inside. She knew—as

women tend to do when it concerns their mate. Jerry had left early that morning on a routine fishing trip out over the bar.

"The weather wasn't bad when he left. . ." she'd said as she closed the door.

"You're right, but a so'wester came in." He held his hat in his hand, fingering the brim as he rotated it in small movements. She knew this was the worst job a policeman had, especially when he knew the victim. She'd had Dan in her Sunday school class; he'd lived just up the street.

"The boat capsized. Jerry helped rescue his crew—told the guys to hang on until the Coast Guard cutter came. And then . . .he. . .well, he didn't come up."

"The others?"

"All accounted for."

The numbness spread through her. "At least he wasn't trapped."

"No, he wasn't."

Laura swallowed hard. "He always said if he had to die at sea, he didn't want to be trapped in the boat."

His eyes didn't quite meet her gaze. "Jerry was a hero, Laura. You need to know that."

Later, after Dan left and her children were there, the tears came. Renee never left her side as neighbors, friends, and her pastor came. Food and flowers were everywhere.

Laura thought about how thankful she was to know that God had been with Jerry. She knew he had drawn comfort from his faith as he died, just as she was now trying to do. The crew couldn't say enough nice things, but nice words didn't bring her husband of twenty years back, nor did nice words lend comfort at night when she reached out to emptiness in the king-sized bed they'd shared.

Renee kept close tabs on her, forcing her to eat. "You have to eat, Laura. You can't sit here all day and stare into space."

That's when the walks started. Even when it rained, she

walked, coming home soaked to the skin. When it was windy she walked, letting the wind push her along, or she fought against it as she turned and came back toward home. She hated the wind as a constant reminder of the accident.

The life and boat insurance policies and investments provided more than adequate money for Laura to live on for the rest of her life, but she knew—had come to realize—that she must do something to feel useful and worthwhile again.

❧

Her mind now went over the ad she'd so carefully composed:

> *Mature woman seeks position as piano player for small church. Experienced. Salary negotiable.*

She'd torn up the first letter and started over. She laughed at the word "mature." What would that mean to most people? And "experienced"—she'd stretched the truth just a bit. She'd played piano for her church in the small farming community where she'd grown up. Since then, she'd always had a piano and had played for her own enjoyment all these years. She'd even given her children lessons.

She jotted down the number and name. *Reverend Gregory Hall, Joseph, Oregon.* She smiled as she tried to put a face with the name.

The door opened and Renee popped in. "Did I hear your phone ring?"

Laura nodded. "Yes, that's why I'm still standing here in sweats with dirt-stained knees. Give me a minute and I'll be there."

"Sure thing." Renee backed out the door. "Your yard's going to be beautiful come fall."

Laura winced as she hurried to the bedroom, choosing navy blue slacks and a pale blue sweatshirt. Mornings were still cool in March. She ran a brush through her short brown hair and decided against makeup. She'd do that before going to the post office for her mail.

She walked across the yard and into Renee's house, wondering if she'd ever enjoy baking again. She hadn't baked after Jerry died, not even for the kids. The two younger ones had still been at home, while Kurt was in his first year of college. Now Kurt had graduated and managed a marine supply house, while Jen was chasing down a career in Seattle. Steve, the youngest, had decided to travel before entering college.

Laura sniffed the air. "I love scones, as you well know."

Pale blue living room walls gave way to splashes of orange and yellow in Renee's large country-style kitchen. The tea-kettle hummed on the stove, the lemony fragrance filling the kitchen.

Renee indicated a chair. "I think it's time we talk, and it always goes better over a cup of tea."

"Talk? What about?"

"Okay." Renee looked exasperated. "We've been friends for a good many years. If you can't talk to me, who can you talk to?"

Laura liked Renee—she'd do anything for a friend, but she was often pushy and would keep at Laura until she found out what she wanted to know. Besides, Laura never could hide her emotions.

"You've been acting funny this past week."

"Funny?" Laura poured a scant teaspoon of sugar into her tea. "In what way?"

"Hey." Her friend reached over and grabbed Laura's arm. "This is me, Renee. Your buddy. The one you share your life with. I know something is going on and want to know what." Renee's round face looked serious, her gaze meeting Laura's. "We haven't been friends for fifteen years for nothing."

Laura swallowed hard as she bit into her buttered scone. "It's time to move on, to do something with my life."

"What? Did you say move on?" Renee sputtered, sending bits of scone across the kitchen table. "Excuse me, but did I hear right?"

Laura nodded, looking at her friend over the rim of her teacup.

"Didn't I just see you planting dahlias?"

"I know. I do things like that to keep busy. That's the whole point. I need more in my life right now than planting flowers, reading books, volunteering, TV, and waiting for a man who will never come home." The last words came out in a squeak.

"Oh, honey." Renee put her arm around Laura. "I know it's been hard."

"No, you don't know. Nobody does until they've gone through it. Even the pastor, with all his wisdom, can't know."

Renee said nothing.

"I still set two cups for coffee each morning, buy the T-bones Jerry liked so well. . ."

Renee nodded. "You're right. I can't pretend to know. If something happened to Derek—" She stood back. "But I can't believe you've been thinking about this without a word to me."

"I know. I wanted to tell you a hundred times, but I feel foolish about the whole thing. Why would I leave the only home I've known for twenty-four years to move to a small mountain town four hundred miles away? It doesn't make sense, nor is it logical."

"Since when is logic any fun?" Renee poured more tea from her favorite teapot, an heirloom from her father's side. "My concern is losing a dear neighbor and friend."

"I'll always be your friend, no matter what."

"I know." Renee touched Laura's hand. "So, where is this place?"

"The Wallowas in the northeast corner of Oregon. It's beautiful. It's also Nez Perce country. Jerry and I visited years ago. Ever been there?"

Renee shook her head. "You know me and Derek are just ol' homebodies."

"That phone call was from a pastor answering one of my ads." Laura trembled as she said it, still not quite believing that someone would answer her ad.

"An ad for what?"

"A job. What else?"

"A job? What kind of a job are you talking about?"

"Part-time, playing the piano. I've kept my piano skills up. Why not use them?"

Renee nodded. "That you have. So, what did this pastor say?"

"Didn't get to the phone in time."

Renee put another scone on Laura's plate. "Then you'd better call him back."

"You think I should?"

"If you've gone this far, you don't want to stop now."

Laura breathed a sigh of relief. "You're the first to know of my plans."

"I gathered that."

"Kurt will be okay. He's got his job, and that keeps him busy on the road two weeks out of four. Then there's Susan. She loves him dearly."

"And the other two are settled. For now," Renee added. "What about the house?"

"I'll leave it empty for the time being. This may not pan out."

Renee kept stirring her tea. "Can't help but think I don't want it to. When would you leave?"

"I'm not sure." Laura downed her second cup of tea and put the rest of the scone in her napkin. "I need to get back now."

"You mean before we talk this through."

"There's nothing to talk through?"

"Oh, yes, there is." Renee grabbed a notebook and pen. "We need to make a list."

"A list? Isn't it a bit late?" But even as she said it, she knew it was futile. Renee was methodical. She shopped with lists, cleaned her house by a list, and made all major decisions after consulting a list.

"I'll number the advantages." Renee wrote the date across the top of the paper. "Then we'll number the disadvantages." Renee ran a hand through her short sandy hair. "You need to do this with any decision: moving, whether you want a baby, a new husband—"

"Hold it!" Laura pushed her chair back. "I get the point, but I'm just not ready for lists or husbands." Laura always thought through decisions carefully. She'd talk about buying a new living room sofa and start looking two months later. Renee would shop one day, and the next morning it would be delivered.

"Thanks, 'Nee, but I'm going home. Talk to you later."

"Here. Was going to give you these anyway since they're your favorites." She handed over a bag filled with three scones. "Be sure to keep me posted on everything."

"I will. I promise."

Laura thought of the message as she made her way back across the yard. The voice had been deep and confident. What was the person like inside? Was she really opening a can of worms? Was this a good choice? She needed to call back, discuss the possible job opening, and see what the pastor's expectations were.

She entered the house, glanced at Jerry's picture on the fireplace mantel, and blew him a kiss. "Honey, I've got to do this. I hope you understand. I'm going to answer this message. For the first time in a long while, I'm looking forward to what tomorrow will bring." She threw her arms wide open. "Lord, I will do this if this pastor—whoever he is—wants me. I feel You have led me this far."

The answering machine blinked the numeral two as she entered the house, indicating that another call had come in while she was out. She pushed the *play* button and the same husky voice filled the room.

"In regard to your ad, I thought of something else. There's a good bed-and-breakfast for you to stay in for a while. Should you decide to remain long-term, a small rental house is opening up at the end of May. Just thought this might help you reach a decision."

Laura looked at Jerry's picture again and let her breath out. Was this a good choice? She'd never know if she didn't take that first step. Later there'd be time to decide what to do about the house, Jerry's fishing gear, the furniture, and the accumulation of possessions one acquires after living forever in one spot. Maybe she'd sell. Maybe she'd rent out the house. But first things first. She needed to make the call, see what this Reverend Gregory Hall had in mind.

"Yes," she said aloud. "I can do all things through Christ who strengthens me."

two

Reverend Gregory Michael Hall closed one eye as he stared into the bathroom mirror. Just as he thought. He'd nicked his face shaving. He grabbed toilet paper and dabbed the tiny cut. That's why he preferred a beard: No shaving every morning. A weekly trim sufficed. None of this morning stuff before you had a cup of coffee. Glenn, the best barber in Joseph, had cut his dark hair yesterday and whacked off most of the beard before shaving his face smooth.

"Looks like it's time to give you a shave, Reverend. When the cherry blossoms are blooming in town, the beard goes." It was a spring ritual. No man in Joseph wore a beard during the spring and summer months.

Cobalt blue eyes stared back from the bathroom mirror. The woman—Laura Madison—would arrive today. He had no idea when. He hadn't been able to pin her down. She'd said it all depended on when she left Sealand.

Gregory had made arrangements for her to stay at Ruth's Mountain View Bed & Breakfast. Ruth had opened almost the first "B & B" in Joseph, a huge house on the ridge. Tourists liked the view of the Wallowa Mountains, yet it was close enough to walk into town. Ruth always had a guest room ready, as she had three bedrooms on the second floor and two on the top. She never tired of having guests and would welcome Laura Madison with open arms.

The early morning sun peeked up over the mountain, nearly blinding him with its brilliance. Soon the snow would melt. It was already gone from the valley's low places, but patches clung to the higher spots. Gregory knew he would never tire of the picturesque scene: the lush, verdant valleys fed by clear mountain streams and the wild daisies dotting the meadows each summer. Mornings were crisp, some downright cold, but by noon the sun penetrated the little town.

Gregory liked Joseph in the spring. It was the best time of year. The boys liked it because school would soon be out. He found himself wishing he had someone to share this glorious time of year with. If only—

Gregory wouldn't think of the if onlys. *God, I have much to be thankful for. My boys. My church. The people here. I love them all. And if my heart is a bit lonely, so be it.*

Standing in a T-shirt, he ran a hand through his unruly, thick hair. Thank heaven for Scandinavian ancestors. His father was buried with a full head of snow-white hair. Gregory's had streaks of gray and someday it would turn white.

The boys clattered down from the loft where they shared one large dorm room the whole length of the house. Soon they would leave for school. Joel, the eldest, a seventh grader who was almost thirteen, acted like he was going on thirty. Serious-minded, he was also getting fussy about his appearance, needing to comb his blond hair several times before he was satisfied. His pickiness and his reluctance to do things with the family bothered Gregory. He remembered being that way, but he had never been as quiet or reserved as Joel. It was only in later years that he grew quiet and reflective.

"Dad! Aren't you through in there?"

Gregory glanced at his watch. The bus didn't come for twenty minutes.

"Be just another minute."

"You say that every morning."

"Don't say anything back," Gregory muttered under his breath. Though he was annoyed, he kept his retorts to himself as they did nothing to improve the boy's disposition.

He buttoned his navy blue corduroy shirt, his heart swelling at the memory of watching his eldest being born. It had truly been one of life's greatest moments to see that tiny bit of humanity, the fingers clutching his so fiercely.

Gregory couldn't believe it had been nine years since the boys' mother had died. It had happened so fast. An aneurysm following childbirth was rare but not unheard of, the doctor at the hospital in Enterprise had said. "I'm so sorry, Reverend Hall."

❧

When Gregory had come to Joseph, fresh out of seminary, young and unattached, he thought he was destined to stay that way. The district superintendent had other ideas. "You need to consider marrying," he said. "A pastor needs a wife, and the congregation needs him to have one."

Gregory nodded in agreement. He knew it to be true, but getting over the woman he had loved—who had jilted him— still consumed him. It had been the worst tragedy of his young life. Beth Marie was constantly in his thoughts. Somehow he couldn't think of dating anyone just yet.

Three months later, Shirley Bishop, who worked at the local café, volunteered to help out at the church one day a week. She printed the weekly bulletins and answered his mail. He soon looked forward to her bright smile and sunny disposition, and she helped him get acquainted with the members of the small church. Feeling indebted to her, he asked her to dinner one night, and, since they seemed congenial, he asked her out again. One thing led to another, and soon they made plans to marry. He loved and respected Shirley, but didn't feel the all-consuming love he'd had for Beth Marie. Still, he felt God had led him to this step. Besides, everyone in Joseph thought this girl, with her scattering of freckles and happy-go-lucky smile, was just right for Preacher Hall. Caleb, the youngest, was a constant reminder of his mother.

Shirley had made him a good home, played piano for the

small congregation, and taught a Sunday school class. He hadn't realized until after her death how much he actually loved his wife. Even now, after nine years, he missed her. . . . Yet he had never quite forgotten Beth Marie. It was a different feeling, and he decided it was okay.

Since Shirley's death, their boys were the one thing that kept him going, made him work hard, and made him forget his loneliness.

❧

"Dad!" Joel banged on the door. "The bus comes in ten minutes."

"Eighteen," he muttered under his breath.

"Dad!"

"Okay! It's all yours!"

Joel glared as he pushed his way past his father. "I told you we needed another bathroom."

"I thought that was only necessary with girls."

"Yeah. Right."

Gregory entered the kitchen and put the coffee on. Mornings weren't complete without at least two cups.

"Mornin', Dad," Caleb called. He was lacing his shoes and had his backpack on the floor beside him.

"Good morning, yourself," Gregory answered. "Your school conference is tomorrow, right?"

"Yes, Dad," he sighed. "I wrote it on the calendar."

Caleb opened the front door, paused, then came back and kissed his father's cheek. "See ya after school."

"Yeah, sure."

Gregory smiled inwardly. Sometimes he felt as if he were a child and his boys were the father. They admonished him a lot. Of course, he had many things on his mind even before he'd read Laura Madison's ad in the *Chieftain*.

The bus honked, the door slammed, and Joel ran out of the bathroom.

"Thanks a lot, Dad! I didn't get to eat breakfast."

"Grab an apple or some bread."

"Never mind."

"Have a good day," he called after the retreating back.

Gregory poured his first cup of coffee and pulled out the nearest chair. He shoved a bowl aside and mopped up a few droplets of milk. Caleb was sloppy, especially in the morning. Joel was fastidious, as Gregory remembered being.

He reached for his old leather Bible. It was a morning for Psalms. About half of the passages were highlighted in fluorescent yellow. His eye caught the first two verses of Psalm 25: "To you, O Lord, I lift up my soul; in you I trust, O my God."

Gregory had often considered moving on from Joseph. He was glad that his church wasn't the sort that changed preachers every three years or so. If the people liked you, you might stay until you retired. But was he doing his job? Was he still an effective minister?

He closed the Bible, said his morning prayer, then rinsed out his cup. Grabbing his denim jacket from beside the door, he hurried out into the morning brightness.

It was a mile into town since he'd moved out on the hill, but he needed to walk. It helped clear his mind and started his day out right. One way that he got close to God was through his daily morning walks. The fresh air made him breathe deeply. His boys were thriving, he had his church family, and those in town who knew him, respected him. Though there were some who never stepped inside his church, he knew most were good people. But that wasn't enough. He had to try harder to win souls.

He reached the end of town and thought again about Shirley. He hadn't given her his all, and he would always regret that.

A car stopped, offering him a ride, but he waved them on. "It's dangerous, Pastor, walking out here with no sidewalks."

Gregory shrugged. "They can see me. Thanks for the offer, brother."

Though he'd had coffee, he hadn't eaten. By the time he reached the middle of town, he was ravenous. He'd stop at the Main Street Café to order another cup of coffee and a slice of cinnamon toast. This wasn't cinnamon toast like his mother made, but a Finnish concoction he'd grown to love. He'd discovered it after first arriving in Joseph. The toast was shipped in from Astoria, Oregon, where a Finnish bakery had been making it since 1910. They sent the special item all over the country.

"This toast is what the sailors took aboard the ships," the owner of the café had told him. "It doesn't mold, rot, or ever taste bad. Just right for dipping into coffee." Since then Gregory's breakfast often consisted of two eggs over easy and three slices of cinnamon toast.

"What's happening today, Reverend?" Sally, the morning waitress, asked. "Anything I need to know about?"

He smiled as he broke the toast in half. "Think we have a piano player coming into town."

"Today?" She didn't need to write the order anymore. In fact, now that he thought about it, Sally never wrote the order. She didn't even carry a pad or pencil in her apron pocket.

"Yes, today. Name is Laura Madison. Says she's mature. Now tell me, Sally, exactly what is 'mature'?"

Sally grinned. "I'd say it's anyone over forty."

"Over forty?" Gregory gulped. "That must mean I'm getting close then."

"You? Never."

"I think it's more like fifty-five or maybe sixty."

"If she's coming today, guess you'll know right soon then."

He dipped his toast into the coffee. "Yep, guess you're right."

After breakfast, Gregory called on old man Kelter, who

still lived alone though he was ninety-three. Gregory enjoyed visiting the salty gentleman, who had a new story to tell each day. Because he worried about him, Gregory looked in on him two or three times a week. He checked his refrigerator, making sure he had enough food, and made sure his feet weren't swelling. Gregory wasn't a doctor, but he knew anyone with diabetes needed to be careful. Kelter hadn't been diagnosed until he was seventy.

&

" 'Old-age diabetes,' the doc said," he had said.

"What's going to happen if you can't cook anymore?" Gregory once asked.

John Kelter had thumped the table. "I ain't ever leavin' this here house and if they take me, I'll run off. Ain't going to no hospital to die like my Clara did. Nosiree!"

&

Gregory found John out in his yard, checking on some bulbs that he'd planted last fall.

"Hi, Preacher!"

"And a top of the morning to you!"

"I heerd tell that a piano player is arriving today."

"How'd you hear that?"

"Word gets around. I may be old and deaf, but I know what's going on."

"Do you want someone to pick you up on Sunday so you can hear her play?"

John squinted as the sun hit the old, crinkled eyes. "Now, Preacher, you know better than to ask me that."

Gregory knew, but that didn't mean he would give up. John was a mountain man in the true sense of the word and worshipped God in his own way. Gregory decided to change the subject.

"Can I take you over to the hospital today or tomorrow for a checkup?"

John squinted again. "No, sir. I have no need for physicals."

"Just thought I'd check."

"I want to die like that Harry Truman did when Mount St. Helen's blew. Die right here in my little house, in my bed or on the sofa, if the good Lord decides that's the best place."

"Okay. I won't bug you about it anymore. Can I bring you dinner one night this week?"

John laughed, revealing a toothless grin. "Now, Preacher, you know the ladies at yore church take care of me real nicelike."

"That's good. Thought they were."

"I'd ask you in, but my favorite game show is coming on in five minutes."

Gregory genially slapped the older man on the back. "I sure wouldn't want to come between you and that game show. I'll see you tomorrow or the next day. And if you're real good, I might bring that piano player around to meet you."

He left the old man standing on his porch, wondering who had encouraged whom. That was the way with the people in this town. They all encouraged and loved one another. He knew he wasn't an outstanding orator, but he was good with his people. It was just relationships with women he failed at.

He turned and headed back downtown to the church that had become his second home.

three

After Laura called Reverend Gregory Hall—"Gregory Michael Hall" he informed her on the phone—they made plans for her to come for an interview the following Tuesday. This gave Laura five days to back out, if she wished.

In those five days she visited old friends. Though it seemed a bit premature, she resigned her positions with the church administrative council, on the library board, as chair of the annual Cancer Walk, and as reading tutor at the local grade school. All were commendable positions: all volunteer jobs to keep her busy, keep her from thinking.

She'd finally worked up her courage to contact her children.

"Mom, this is super!" Jen, her daughter, said. "You need to do something adventuresome for a change. Maybe you'll find a man in Joseph—"

"May I remind you," Laura cut in, "that that is the last thing I hope to do."

"Well, you just never know. But I'm happy for you. I really am. Maybe I'll come over when I have some vacation time."

"I'll send an address as soon as I have one."

She couldn't get in touch with Steve, her vagabond son. He was traveling through Europe, staying at youth hostels. The last she'd heard was that he intended to put off college for at least another six months. Laura was confident that Steve would go with the tide; always did, always had.

She hadn't expected Kurt's reaction, however.

"Mom, is this some stunt you're pulling to get my attention?"

Laura looked at her tall son, so like his father with the same hair coloring, the deep brown eyes that could melt anyone's resolve, the square chin. She wanted to take him into her arms as she had done when he was a child and cuddle him. She'd always had a special feeling for her firstborn. Did other mothers feel this way about the first child?

"I am not trying to prove anything, nor am I trying to get your attention. I'm doing this for me because it's time I did something different."

"Susan and I may get engaged."

"That's wonderful, Kurt. She's a nice, Christian girl."

Kurt and Susan had begun dating way back in junior high when she'd first come to the youth group meetings.

"But you need to be here to—"

"To what? Give you an engagement party?"

"No, not that, but just to be here in case I need advice."

Laura shook her head. "Kurt, I can't always be here for you. You need to make decisions on your own, and I know you're quite capable of doing that."

He sighed as only he could sigh. "You've changed since Dad died."

The words hurt. She'd tried to be a good mother, but it was always as if something important were missing. She'd never been able to explain it, not even to Renee. She stood and faced her son now. "I've done my best by you, Kurt, and you've grown into a responsible young man. You have a good job, a good life, and I trust you to weigh things, to pray about it before making a monumental decision. If Susan is the right mate for you, you'll know."

"Did you pray about this change, Mom?"

She caught the edge in his voice. "I certainly did."

"I just don't like it."

"And maybe I won't, either. Maybe I'll be home in a week or two."

Kurt left with an armful of magazines, a few videos, and food from the refrigerator. "I love you, Mom." He set the stuff down and reached over to hug her. "Whatever you do, be careful."

"I intend to do that very thing."

Laura put off talking to her minister. Pastor Dave Reynolds, at age thirty-two, was graying at the temples. He joked about it often: "It's what happens when you don't let go and let God take care of your life. I was so fearful of going bald, but never thought about going gray."

"This is a big surprise," Dave said when Laura entered his office Monday morning. "I heard about your moving, as one always does in a small town. Guess I didn't want to believe it."

Laura smiled. "Figures. Word travels fast in Sealand."

"Isn't all this resigning a bit premature? What if you don't like it there?"

"Maybe I won't; but if it doesn't work out, I'll move back."

"And the kids. What do they think?"

Laura studied a broken fingernail. "Kurt's the only one with reservations."

Pastor Dave nodded. "Kids want their mothers always to be there and never to change their hairstyle or where they live."

"It's my Sunday dinners he'll miss, not me."

He chuckled. "Yeah. You're probably right on that one. Just be very sure is all I suggest."

Laura nodded. "I am. What's the old saying? 'Nothing ventured, nothing gained'? I guess that's where I'm at right now, Dave."

He walked around his desk. "Good. You sound positive about this step. Some of us get in a rut, and you just happen to be altering your life. We'll miss you. Please keep in touch."

"I'll do that."

"And if you ever need a preacher over that way, give me a holler."

"I'll be sure to tell Pastor Hall."

He put his hand on her shoulder and offered a prayer. Laura thanked him and left.

The final good-bye to Renee wasn't as easy. She'd come over several times already with another list. This last time she'd brought coffee, brownies, and a lunch box filled with goodies for the trip.

"You must remember to turn the heat down, put your phone on vacation status, and—"

"Hold it," Laura interrupted. "I'm not a child."

"Oh, I know. I'm just compulsive. You know that," Renee said, then looked away for a long moment. "I'm going to miss you, kid."

"Then come see me."

"You know we'll never do that, but maybe. . ."

They sat on the deck while they talked and munched on brownies and sipped coffee. The hanging geranium looked bright and made Laura smile. "Here. You might as well take my plant. It isn't going to live without daily watering."

Renee stood, removing the hook from the tree branch. "Thanks. I can use another one at the end of the porch, and this is such a glorious scarlet."

"I'm glad I don't have any animals," Laura said. They'd lost Muffy, an adorable cockapoo, the same year Jerry died, and she hadn't been able to even think of getting a replacement. Just as she hadn't wanted a husband replacement.

Laura always traveled light, so Renee now asked what she was taking.

"Mostly my sweats, some casual pants, sweaters, and a few good outfits."

"They may dress up more there than they do here at the beach."

Laura shrugged. "If so, I'll just have to buy something."

"What about shoes?"

"Two pairs."

"What? Two pairs? You can't get by with two." Renee looked shocked.

"I have my walking shoes and my dress-up ones."

Renee pushed her chair back and shook her head. "You gotta take more. Really. You'll need walking shoes, house shoes, ones you work in, walk in, and at least two for church."

Laura rolled her eyes. "Okay. I'll take more. I'm taking basic black. You have heard of basic black? You suppose that will be suitable?"

"How about a touch of purple or that burgundy you look so good in?"

"I don't think so."

Renee looked at her list and crumpled it up. "I don't know why I try with you. You're going to do your own thing, aren't you?"

Laura bit into a second brownie. "Yes, I guess so. Being mature means you don't have to impress anyone."

"I remember when I saw the one suitcase you took on your trip to Florida."

Laura smiled at the memory. "Yeah, I know, you'd need a suitcase that size just for your lists."

Tears sprang to Renee's eyes. "Who will I have coffee with? Or who will watch a video with me?" Renee often came over while Derek watched some sports program.

"Well, who am I going to have coffee with?"

"You'll find somebody. That's the way you are."

∂•

By Monday night she was prepared, thanks to Renee and her endless lists. Her car's glove compartment held a new, small first aid kit Renee had given her and a flashlight—not a simple one, but one that weighed twenty pounds and flashed in case there was trouble.

"Remember to stay in the vehicle and put this sign in the window." Renee looked fearful. "Don't open your window to anyone except a state patrolman."

"I won't. I promise."

The lunch box contained two sandwiches, cookies, apples and bananas, and a small package of cheese. It was enough for four people. "Are you sure you haven't forgotten something?" Laura asked, trying to conceal her smile. Renee did everything so thoroughly.

"I did!" Renee turned and sprinted across the yard to her house.

"Here!" She ran back, holding up a marked map. "This is the best place to stop to rest and stretch."

"I thought I'd drive straight there."

Renee looked shocked. "Most accidents are caused by the driver being tired or sleepy."

"Relax." Laura leaned over and hugged her friend hard. "I'll stop every other hour. How's that sound?"

"And you'll call when you arrive?"

Laura assured her, "The second I hit town."

They hugged good-bye, as Laura would leave early the next morning. She thought about Renee's statement later. Laura did make friends easily; always had. It was she who had gone over to borrow the proverbial "cup of sugar" from Renee when she moved in.

She finished packing. Just for good measure, and because of what Renee had said, she added a pair of boots. Not exactly dress boots, but they were good for mud should she find any.

Laura could hardly sleep that night as excitement bubbled inside her. She felt young and vibrant at the prospect of exploring new territory. What would tomorrow bring?

During her evening devotion, she stumbled across James 4:13–14: "Now listen, you who say, 'Today or tomorrow we will go to this or that city, spend a year there, carry on business and make money.' Why, you do not even know what will happen tomorrow. What is your life? You are a mist that appears for a little while and then vanishes."

"A mist!" she said aloud. "I am but a mist in the scheme of things." How like God to have a sense of humor, to put a smile on her lips before her new undertaking.

four

The car was packed. One Sunday outfit, a black-and-white houndstooth jacket with solid black skirt—the most slimming outfit Laura owned—hung on the hook. A suitcase with casual clothes and plenty of warm sweaters was in the trunk.

The house looked deserted as she backed out of the driveway. The freshly dug dirt where she'd planted dahlias gave it an incomplete look. "I hope I'm doing the right thing, Jerry," she said, talking to him as if he were right there beside her.

She glanced at Renee's house, but the curtains were still drawn.

Guide me, God, she prayed. *Shield me from all harm. And help me to do what is right.*

Heading over the miles, Laura thought about Renee insisting she call the Wallowa County Visitors' Bureau. "You could get snowbound, you know."

"Yes, it is brisk up in that country the first of April," the lady had said. "There's still snow in the mountains and nights are downright nippy, but if you stay on the main road, you'll be fine. I wouldn't try traveling after dark or too early in the morning." She hesitated. "And stay on the main roads. We lost a car last year and haven't seen it since."

Laura gasped, and the lady chuckled, "I was just kidding, of course."

It might have been better if she'd waited until summer, but the job was open now. There was a need for her, and she knew she had to get away. She felt God leading her in this direction. Laura patted the dashboard. "You'll get me there okay," she said, encouraging the car, "I just know it."

As Laura drove across the Astoria-Megler Bridge, she marveled at the sight. The view was awesome with the Columbia River serene on this clear, windless day. A large ship was anchored east of the bridge, and small fishing boats dotted the water. She doubted she'd ever be able to step foot in a boat again. She'd drive into Portland, then take the I-84 freeway heading east. The freeway ran along the Columbia, past Multnomah Falls, and onto Hood River. At The Dalles, she'd be out of the immense trees and rugged terrain.

Laura listened to gospel music as she drove. "What a mighty God we serve! What a mighty God we serve," she sang lustily. Once, it hit her that she was traveling alone and if something happened, she wasn't sure what she would do; however, she believed in prayer and in guardian angels. Feeling confident, she started another song, "Gentle Shepherd."

An hour later, she stopped for coffee. She'd already eaten one of the sandwiches Renee had packed, but she needed to stretch.

The coffee shop buzzed with activity. It was obviously the place the local people gathered in at The Dalles. A man sat in the large corner booth with cameras flashing as a lady held a microphone in front of him.

"He's our local celebrity," the waitress said as she poured Laura a cup of coffee and handed her a menu. "A state representative, home for Easter."

Laura listened while she had her coffee. The politician glanced her way and smiled. She looked away, deciding against a refill.

Laura topped the tank, then headed east, going through Pendleton, over the Blue Mountains toward La Grande. There she'd turn and go north.

"Can't get lost," the station attendant had said. "You'll hit a couple of small towns on your way to Joseph. Just follow the road signs."

When Laura pulled into Elgin, she looked for a place for

coffee, wishing she'd brought a thermos.

"What's Joseph like?" Laura asked the lady in the bakery while she munched on a maple bar.

"Small town like this one," she responded. She was frosting the sides of a sheet cake. "I been over there once, maybe twice." She glanced up. "Why? You goin' to move there?"

Laura nodded. "I might."

"Where you coming from?"

"The Washington coast."

"And you're moving here?"

Laura sipped her coffee. She supposed it did sound strange. "Let's just say I need a change."

The lady nodded. "I felt that way when I left Oklahoma."

Laura smiled. "Thought I detected an accent."

"Moved here ten years ago and love it. Small town atmosphere. If you're in a hurry, this is not the place to live."

"I know what you mean." Laura poured another cup of coffee since the pot was close and she didn't want to take the woman away from her cake. "I come from a small place now. I like small. I want to know my neighbor and my neighbor's neighbor."

"It'll be like that in Joseph, for sure."

"What's the picture on the computer screen?"

"That's what's going on the top of this cake."

"It is?" Laura stepped closer, studying the photo.

"Yep. New way of decorating cakes. She pointed to a small machine next to the computer. "People send photos and I put them on the cake. If you wait a sec, you'll see that photo right on top of this cake."

Laura waited.

"Saw how to do this on the Internet and decided to try it. Bought the scanner, and now that's the only kind of decorating people want. This here cake is heading to Portland via UPS. Got an order from a lady up there."

A voice came on the computer, saying the scanner was ready. Laura watched as the cake inched ever so slowly under the scanner.

"Voila! Here it is."

"I must get a picture." Laura zoomed in on the cake and took two photos to make sure at least one would turn out. "If I ever need a cake for a special occasion, I'll be sure to call."

"Joseph isn't exactly close, you know."

"It's a lot closer than Portland." Laura put her camera back in the case and thanked the baker for the demonstration.

She left and wended her way north. On the drive out of Elgin, the flat valley soon gave way to forested hills, then the snow-topped Wallowa Mountains.

Laura pulled off in a turnaround, got out, and inhaled deeply the crisp mountain air. She took a photo to send Renee and the kids, then got back in. Already she knew she'd need a heavier coat than the one she'd brought.

The Wallowa River meandered along the road and fishermen in hip boots, heavy coats, and caps with earflaps lined the riverbank. She waved at one who held up a good-sized fish, and a lump came to her throat. Though Jerry had only fished once with waders in a stream, it brought back poignant memories of that time, and she wondered if they might not have come here again to fish. She'd have to find out what they were catching. At home it was mostly salmon. Boats went out beyond the bar for tuna and bottom fish; some fished for sturgeon from the bank.

Going through more small towns, heading south, Laura felt she was backtracking, but it couldn't be helped. She had the map Renee had marked so well, and there was clearly only one road into Joseph. If she could have cut across from La Grande, the route would have been more direct.

Enterprise was the closest town to Joseph. Laura drove by the courthouse, admiring the large building and sprawling lawn. She got out of the car and stretched her legs. She decided to walk over to a mall, where she found a chamber of commerce and picked up maps and literature about the area.

Laura arrived in Joseph at four. She hadn't figured it would take all day, but neither had she figured she'd be stopping every ten minutes to snap another photo. It wasn't determined that she'd move here; it might be the only time she'd come this way. She wanted pictures to show everyone back home.

A pair of magnificent bronzed horses graced the lawn of a large factory. She'd heard about the bronzed sculptures that were shipped all over the world. She'd have to take a tour after she settled in.

ᵥ

It was too late to find the Reverend Gregory Michael Hall in the church office. He'd be home by now. Or would he be waiting for her? Maybe his wife had cooked dinner and she'd be asked to join them. But she did need to freshen up a bit first and, of course, call Renee.

A bookstore caught her eye on the right, and it seemed to be attached to several other buildings comprising a mall. The restroom sign was a most welcome sight.

Her hair was flying in every direction. That's what happened when you drove with the window at half-mast. She looked tired, with bags under her eyes. It had been a full day. Perhaps Reverend Hall wouldn't notice. She was coming to fill a position, not be scrutinized for her looks.

After applying fresh makeup, Laura stopped in the bookstore. The lady was just turning the "Open" sign around.

"Please excuse me," Laura called out. "I know it's late, but I'm looking for this place." She handed her the address scribbled in her address book.

The woman nodded. "That would be Pastor Hall's home. He's out on the Joseph highway, about a mile. New place. Sits up on the hill. Looks out over the river and Chief Joseph's Cemetery."

"Oh. It's not in town, then?"

"Not quite, but close. Hey, I'm Nancy."

"Laura Madison."

"Are you the lady who placed an ad in the *Chieftain?* Everyone was talking about it."

"Figures you'd already know about me," Laura said.

"We read every line of the paper, you know."

"I'm coming to play the piano at the Community Church. Do you go there?"

Nancy held out a business card. "I live in Enterprise, and coming down here six days a week is enough."

"Do you know Reverend Hall?"

"Oh, yes. Small town, you know. Everyone knows everyone. You'll soon discover that. Reverend Hall comes in often. Nice enough man, but—"

"But?"

"It's nothing. No, I like him. He's friendly."

Laura still wondered what the "but" referred to as she picked up a book on the counter.

"I'd let you look around, but I'm closing early. School board meeting tonight."

"That's fine. I don't have time to browse now, anyway. But later. I'm an avid reader."

"Good. Here, do you want this coffee? I was going to dump it out. I also have a pizza roll, one of our specialties. They're very popular with the locals."

"Why, thank you." Laura took the coffee and roll. "I am a bit hungry. Never stopped for lunch."

"You're staying the night, of course."

"Yes, at a bed-and-breakfast."

"That would be Ruth's Mountain View."

"Is it a good place?"

"Ruth's the best. Marvelous cook, too." She turned the lights off except for one. "You just go on out there. Can't miss it. There's a fence around the house. He has a dog, you know."

"Thanks for the directions and the coffee and roll."

Laura drove slowly through town, looking at the small cafés, motels, museum, and gas station. It was pretty small, smaller than she'd thought. Enterprise was definitely the larger town of the two.

Laura looked east to the line of mountains. She knew she would never tire of the scene and could hardly wait to explore the area. A road sign pointed to Wallowa Lake. Everyone had told her not to miss the lake. "Even if you're there just a day, you must go to the lake and stop at the small country store. Has the best fudge ever." This from her pastor whom she'd called the night before leaving.

She then saw the sign to the cemetery. Looking to her left, she couldn't miss the house. It sat on a small knoll with a commanding view of the cemetery, the lake, and the hills on the eastern edge. She turned on her signal and climbed the driveway that wound up and around.

She heard barking from within and waited for someone to answer the doorbell. A young boy soon appeared. "Are you the piano lady coming from Washington?" The boy had a rash of freckles across his face and a happy-go-lucky smile.

She nodded. "That I am."

"My name's Caleb. C'mon in."

"Hello, Caleb." Laura stepped inside and shook his hand. "I'm Laura Madison. Are your parents home?"

His smile froze. "Parents? You mean my dad?"

"Well, yes, your dad. And I thought, well—"

"Don't have a mother, you know. She died when I was born."

"Oh." Laura let the shock sink in. "I didn't know. I am so

sorry." What else could you say to a child when you've assumed he has a mother? "I guess you'd better take me to your father then."

five

Caleb closed the door just as a small, woolly dog raced around the corner and jumped up on her.

"Down, Patsy!" Caleb grabbed the wriggling bundle. "She loves company."

"Caleb, put the dog in your bedroom."

Laura glanced up from petting the excited dog as the man owning the voice entered the room, extending his hand. "Laura Madison?"

"Yes." She offered her hand, and he shook it heartily. "I was expecting you earlier and also expecting someone more —what was the word in your ad?"

"Mature?"

"Yes, mature."

Laura often felt every bit of her forty-five years but was told she looked and acted younger. She could see she had already failed on two counts. The man looked older than he probably was, but it was the brooding eyes that caught her attention. She trembled before answering.

"You were expecting someone with gray hair. Well, I am mature in nature, if not age, and I arrived late because I kept stopping to take pictures."

"I see. You must be a camera buff, then." He ran a hand through his thick mop of dark hair.

Laura nodded. "I met Nancy at the bookstore, and she directed me here."

"We do have a great bookstore. Big selection." His eyes met her gaze. "We can still talk, of course, but tomorrow morning would be a better time."

"Of course." Laura looked away. Reverend Hall was taller than she'd even imagined, and his eyes were deep blue and penetrating. She wasn't sure what she'd expected, but not someone nearly this handsome. He looked as if he belonged in these rugged mountains. His presence unnerved her and she wasn't quite sure why. It wasn't as if he'd lied to her. He just hadn't told her he was a widower.

"I think there's been a mistake—that is—on my part."

"A mistake?"

She looked at Caleb, who'd returned, then back at Reverend Hall. "I assumed you had a wife."

"Oh." He chuckled just as a blast sounded down the hall. Laura jumped.

"That's Joel practicing his horn," Caleb offered. "He practices two hours a day."

"Yes, well, I'm sure Mrs. Madison doesn't need to know all our habits. Would you go check on the hamburgers, Son?" He turned back to Laura. "Guess I forgot to mention that I'm a widower."

Laura tried to smile. "I suppose that doesn't change your need for a pianist."

"It certainly doesn't. We're in dire need, especially this Sunday, as we have new members joining, and I like to have special music. I thought of having a pianist come over from Enterprise, but she'd arrive late and what is a service without the introit?"

Laura felt uncomfortable, almost inconsequential in this man's presence, and wasn't sure why. It was evident that he ran his household with a firm hand.

"I meant to arrive before mealtime."

"Dinner is early because of Caleb's game. Second of the season. Now we'll be on a schedule of early dinners." He turned, raking his hand through his hair again. She decided it had to be his nervous habit.

"Is that baseball?" Laura hadn't realized it was that time of year already.

"Yes. Do you enjoy the game?"

Laura nodded again. "My sons played. I've spent my share of time at the ball field."

"Perhaps you'd like to join us for a hamburger and potato chips. Nothing fancy, but it'd be a way to meet the boys and we can talk about the position."

Before Laura could respond, "Yankee Doodle" sounded from the bedroom.

"He plays well, doesn't he?" she said.

"His face would turn red if he knew you were here listening to him," Caleb offered, looking at her expectantly.

"Dinner?" Reverend Hall repeated.

"Yes, that would be lovely. I even have a pizza roll to add to the table. Since it's so large, we can divide it four ways."

"Go put on an extra plate and don't forget the napkin," the reverend said to Caleb.

The music stopped and a lanky boy with a scowl appeared in the living room, his head down. "Dad, do I have to go to the game—" He stopped when he saw Laura. "Didn't know we had company."

"This is Mrs. Madison, Joel. Laura, this is Joel, my eldest son. Remember I told you she was coming to play the piano since Gert isn't coming back to Joseph and Amanda just didn't work out?"

"Yeah." He thrust his hands in the pockets of his Levis. "I remember."

"A gentleman offers his hand," the reverend said.

Joel stepped forward, his eyes not meeting Laura's. His hand was limp, but she added firmness to her shake. "You can really play the trumpet."

His face flushed as he hurried from the room.

"He's an okay kid, but needs some refining. . . ."

"That comes later, perhaps, Reverend," Laura said.

"Gregory. You may call me Gregory. No need for formality."

Caleb hollered from the kitchen. "I think these hamburgers are done, Dad!"

Laura smiled. Reverend Hall might teach Joel formal manners, but Caleb was another story. "Could I possibly help in some way?"

"Everything's done," Caleb said, coming back into the room with a uniform on.

"Wow, that was quick," Laura said. Caleb's eyes lit up his whole face, and Laura realized why she had come here. Yes, she'd play the piano for a small community church, but there were two motherless boys who might need her presence more.

Gregory left the room. Laura followed Caleb, having the first feeling of acceptance.

"Of course you're coming to my baseball game," Caleb announced as they entered a kitchen. With pale green walls and an apple border, everything was immaculate, not what one expected in a house without a woman. She pulled out a chair.

"Now, Son, Mrs. Madison is too tired to go to your game."

Gregory glanced over as Laura blurted out, "But I'd like to go. Really, I would."

"Good, then I don't have to," Joel said, shuffling into the room.

"Now, Son, we've had this discussion before."

"I don't want to go."

"Dad, he doesn't have to—"

"He's going and that's final. I'll hear no more about it." Gregory bowed his head. "Let's thank God for this meal."

"If I fail English, it's your fault!"

"Joel! Enough. There'll be time for studying after the game."

The younger boy pushed his chair back and dumped his plate in the sink.

Laura had only finished half her hamburger. She'd forgotten

how quickly men and young boys ate. "These are certainly delicious. I need the recipe," she said, feeling uncomfortable.

Gregory laughed. "Just chopped up onions and a dash of ketchup."

"They're so moist."

"I like them that way, and the boys don't care as long as it's food. When their mother died, I couldn't make anything but macaroni and cheese dinners."

"And noodles?"

"No. They didn't like those much, especially the one combination I tried."

"What was that?"

"Leftover split pea soup and chicken noodle; I combined the two."

Laura made a face. "Oh. I don't think I'd like it, either."

"And you threw in leftover rice, Dad." Caleb was back in the room, lacing up his shoes. "It was the grossest ever!"

Laura tried to keep a straight face. It had been so long since her children had been young. She'd forgotten how picky they were, but one could never fail with hamburgers, hot dogs, and pizza. Her Kurt hadn't even liked turkey.

The kitchen was cleaned in minutes while Caleb grabbed his mitt and cap.

"We'll direct you to Ruth's right after the game," Gregory said, holding the back door open for her. "We'll come back here to get your car, if that's okay."

"Sounds fine."

"You'll love Ruth. Everyone does," Gregory said.

Laura met his steady gaze. "She sounds like the town's grandma. We have a grandmotherly type back in Sealand. Her name's Dorothy. She never married, so the church is her family. If you miss a Sunday, she calls to see if you're ill. She keeps track of everyone from her seat in the back row."

"Does Dorothy make cookies?" Caleb asked, punching his

hand into his baseball mitt. "Ruth bakes the best chocolate chip cookies of anyone I know."

Gregory nodded. "Yes, but I prefer her peanut butter. I agree that she's the best cook this side of the Rockies. Her cookies are the first to disappear when we have the annual Christmas cookie walk."

"Does she have other specialties?" Laura asked.

"I'd say 'to die for.' " Gregory smiled. Laura realized it was the first time a smile had crossed his face since she met him. "We go to her place Sundays after church for brunch."

"Waffles," Caleb said. "And blueberry pancakes."

"Canadian bacon, hash browns, and fruit compote," Gregory added.

"She doesn't make anything like noodles and pea soup," Caleb said.

"We should get along just fine then." Laura smiled. There was something about this kid she liked, really liked. He so reminded her of Kurt and his exuberance at that age. She noticed Joel hadn't said a word during the exchange, and her heart went out to him.

❧

The baseball field immediately brought back pleasant memories. Boys in uniform were dashing around while the coach told them to pay attention. Pitchers were practicing their throws. Laura thought about Kurt playing up through the Babe Ruth League. Playing left field, he dove for fly balls and hit the ball hard when up to bat. She sighed. What had happened to that sweet, eager child? Nearly engaged to be married to a wonderful girl, he seemed morose, totally unhappy, as if he were searching for something.

The evening was cool and she was glad she'd worn the heavy sweater and brought along her coat.

"Hi, Reverend Hall," the coach called out. "Maybe this is the night that Caleb hits a home run."

Gregory made the victory sign. "He'll come around."

"Is this the new piano player you been advertising for?" The coach leaned over the fence, and Laura had to laugh as she was introduced. Everyone knew about her coming, even the coach.

Gregory left for the concession stand, returning with peanuts, a bag of popcorn, and two long raspberry ropes. "Have to support the team, you know. I work the concession stand one Saturday a month. Little League is big in Joseph, in case you hadn't guessed." He smiled as their eyes met. Laura trembled unexpectedly as she took the popcorn.

"I'm used to the life of a Little League mother." She popped a kernel in her mouth. "I, too, did the concession stand. We had hot dogs for fifty cents then."

"Did you want a hot dog?" he asked.

"Heavens, no, not after that wonderful meal."

Gregory eased back on the stadium seat. It was funny how Laura felt herself going into this phase. It had nearly taken her back ten years to those days when Jerry rushed home from work and met her at the ball field. Most times she had something in the slow cooker, so they would eat the second they got home.

"Your children played ball, then?"

Laura nodded. "Kurt, the oldest, played every sport he could, but baseball was his favorite. He plays on a local softball team now."

"That's one thing parents usually have in common—an interest in the local sports. Joseph people are wonderful at supporting the community, especially school activities."

"It's important," Laura agreed. "How about the churches? Would you say most people are Christian?"

"Definitely." Greg glanced at Caleb, who was up at bat. "Caleb's been in a batting slump, couldn't hit during practice or the game last week, but he'll pull out of it."

The young boy hunched over the plate, winging his bat as

he got into a crouched position.

"I have an idea he's going to hit that ball over the fence," Laura said just as the first ball came down the pike.

Cra-a-ack! Caleb slammed the first pitch far into right field, not over the fence, but far enough to bring the first batter in as he darted around the bases to third on a stand-up.

Laura jumped to her feet, clapping and cheering while the team made high fives.

"How about that?" Gregory said after everyone sat down. "He's over his slump."

Laura then noticed she'd dumped over the full bag of popcorn. She laughed as she looked at the golden puffs down on the ground. "I always have been a klutz," she murmured.

"What's a little popcorn?" Gregory asked. "Do you want more?"

"No, I think not. I have an idea I'm not going to be sitting long enough to eat any. Now, a red rope I can nibble on."

An ecstatic Caleb ran to the bleachers to hug his father, though he wasn't supposed to leave the dugout. "I did it, Dad! I finally hit the ball!" He hugged Laura impulsively. "Wasn't that the greatest hit ever, Laura? I mean, Mrs. Madison?" The freckles on his nose seemed to dance.

She ruffled his hair. "That's okay. You can call me Laura. And, yes, it was a smashing hit." For the first time in a very long while, she felt good inside.

"Happy is he who trusts in the Lord," Laura said then.

Gregory cast a glance in her direction and finally nodded. "I'd say that's a good assessment, Mrs. Madison."

six

The inning was over and the Blue Chiefs won: 7–6. The parents cheered, pounding each other on the back. A scowling Joel strode up.

"Wasn't that a great game?" Caleb asked his older brother. His gaze was expectant.

"Not as good as last week's—"

"Now, Joel," Gregory interrupted, "just because you don't play baseball is no reason—"

"I'd never play that stupid game. We have to in P. E., and it gags me then."

Laura tried not to notice the disappointment cross Caleb's face or the disgust on Gregory's. She remembered sibling rivalry, how the younger child looked up to the older, always hoping for a few words of praise. It had been that way with her sons, and she saw the same thing happening here, though she didn't know these boys yet.

"Well, I didn't see last week's game," Laura said then, "so I have no way of comparing. I thought it was a wonderful hit and two stupendous catches." She paused momentarily. "Now I'm looking forward to seeing what you do best, Joel." For a brief moment the older boy smiled, but his face froze, as if it was against the rules to be pleased with himself.

"Joel mainly plays trumpet," Caleb said, looking over his shoulder as he hurried back over to his team to help pick up the equipment.

"Playing trumpet is no easy task," Laura said. "It takes a lot of lung power. My youngest son played in the band—"

"Your kids were busy," Gregory broke in.

"Have you played for church?" Laura asked, ignoring Gregory's comment. Sudden inspiration hit.

"No," Gregory said, answering for his son. "Joel isn't much for playing in public. No solos, that is."

Joel scowled. Before she could say anything, he turned and looked in the other direction. She didn't like it when parents spoke for their children. From the looks of things, Gregory had been answering for his eldest son for quite some time now.

" 'God of Our Fathers' is a beautiful piece with a trumpet solo," Laura interjected. "It shows off the trumpet nicely."

"I don't think he'd do it."

We shall see, Laura thought, knowing she'd need to approach this slowly.

"Let's go for ice cream at the Wallowa Lake General Store," Gregory announced. "And then I'll lead you to Ruth's."

"Caleb?"

"He'll go with his team. They go to the café on Main Street."

The sun was setting, but the night was beautiful and invigorating. "I've been eager to see the lake."

"You should go during the day," Joel grunted from the backseat.

Greg pulled up in front of a brown building. "This is the place."

A deer was licking up the remains of a dropped ice cream cone.

"Oh, how sweet," Laura exclaimed.

"Don't get too close," Gregory warned. "You've got to be careful with the deer. Those hind legs can really kick and make you hurt for weeks."

"But they're so tame," Laura exclaimed. "I've never seen deer come right up to you like that."

"That's because they get fed. Heaven help them if they had to go out and forage for real food."

"Hey, Reverend," Oliver called out from inside the store. "Haven't seen you in a week or so."

"Been busy." He turned toward Laura. "Oliver, this is Laura Madison, our new piano player at church. You'll have to come hear her play."

Laura extended her hand.

"Pleased to meet you. And this is my wife, Keithanne."

A short woman with a round, pleasant face smiled. "Happy to meet you, and welcome to the lake."

"It's a beautiful spot." Laura had noticed the lake all the way out. It was so calm and pristine. She wondered if they had storms here that would beat the water up into a frenzy as it did at home.

"I hope you like it here," Keithanne said.

"It's going to be totally different for her," Gregory said. "From the ocean to the mountains."

"Yeah. From beach bum to mountain gal," Laura said, looking around. The store carried a bit of everything one could ever want. "Nice store."

"Thanks," they both chorused.

Laura stared at the trays of fudge. Mocha almond fudge, amaretto, maple nut, chocolate walnut, and more.

"Here, have a sample." Oliver cut off a tiny slab. Laura tried the fudge walnut, then a piece of peanut butter. "Made with fresh Dutch cream," he said proudly.

"It's all so good."

Keithanne had already scooped a cone for Gregory. She looked at Laura. "Ice cream or fudge?"

"Ice cream, definitely. But I want fudge to send to my best friend in Sealand."

She chose chocolate peanut butter ice cream in a waffle cone and mocha almond fudge for Renee. "My friend will be surprised to get this from me so soon," Laura said with a laugh.

"We'd better head back," Gregory said. Joel was already in the car.

There were two deer waiting now. "Don't even look at them," Gregory said.

"But, look, one is crippled."

"Yeah, he's been around for a long time now, crippled at birth," Keithanne said from the doorway.

Joel was in the car, munching away on his thick slab of fudge.

"Do you always get fudge instead of ice cream?" Laura asked.

He grunted an answer, which she couldn't quite determine. She would just let it drop; but more than anything, she wanted to be friends with this young boy. Maybe if she continued to talk to him, he'd come around.

It was dusk and Laura could barely see the lake. "This is such beautiful country. I don't remember much about the lake when Jerry and I came years ago."

"It's stayed pretty much the same," Gregory offered. "Did you know there is not one signal light in Wallowa County?"

"There isn't?" Even in her small area at the beach, there were signal lights, one in each town. "Never have been?"

"No, and never will be if we can keep the developers out."

"I hope it never changes. It's beautiful as it is. I wouldn't want it to change in the least bit."

"Tell that to our congressman, then."

Laura thought of the man she'd seen in The Dalles. He looked like a progressive congressman. She wondered if he was behind the potential growth plan for this secluded spot in northeast Oregon.

"How do people make a living here?"

"Tourism," Joel announced from the backseat. "Farming. Some cattle. Lots of mint. No logging."

"There's not much logging anymore," Laura said.

"Yeah. People have to find other ways to make money," Gregory said. "I've seen change since I first arrived and I wish it could stay the same."

"But if people don't have jobs, Dad, they'll have to move on, and then there won't be enough for a church and you'll have to leave, anyway."

Gregory shook his head. "My son, the realist."

"Somebody has to think about the future," Joel said, slouching further into his seat.

Laura finished the last of her ice cream and wondered about the universe. She recycled and had once joined the "Save Our Seals" campaign.

"We're going home, aren't we, Dad?" Joel asked with a scowl. Laura wondered if he ever smiled.

"Yes. We need to stop at the house for Mrs. Madison's car."

After dropping Joel off and getting her own car, Laura followed Gregory back into town, turning right and going up a hill to a house at the end of the road.

The Victorian house, a creamy white with gray gingerbread trim and a wraparound porch, made Laura feel she was going back in time. She could hardly wait to see inside.

Gregory got out and walked over to her car. "Can I help carry something in?"

Closing her trunk, she pointed to her larger suitcase and grabbed the smaller one, then followed him across the lawn and up the steps. The white picket fence around the yard reminded Laura of her grandmother's farmhouse.

A light shone from an old-fashioned porch light. "It's perfectly lovely."

As if waiting for her arrival, a small woman opened the door and peered out. "Well, are you coming in, Pastor, or staying out there all night?"

After introductions, Ruth put her arms around Laura. "I'm the hugging type, dear. I do hope you don't mind. But come in and have a spot of tea. It's a delightful country blend. And freshly baked peanut butter cookies." She reached up to hug Gregory. "Do set the suitcase down in the hall, first." Wisps of gray hair framed her face. She wore a white apron over a flowered housedress. Laura thought that she looked exactly the part of a bed-and-breakfast matron.

Gregory shook his head. "Sounds wonderful, Ruth, but I've got to get home. Big day tomorrow." He glanced at Laura. "I'll expect you in my office at nine in the morning."

"Gregory, be reasonable. Laura must be exhausted. She may want to sleep in, you know."

He looked almost chagrined. "Oh, yes. Well, whenever you make it, that's fine."

After Gregory left, Laura accepted the offer of tea. "We just had ice cream at a wonderful little store by the lake. I feel as if I've done nothing but eat since arriving."

Ruth's eyes twinkled. "You went to the Boeves' then. Yes, it's a delightful place. Great people."

Laura looked at the forest green walls with touches of lavender and rose. Bay windows looked out onto the front yard. "I love it," Laura said.

"Wait until you see your room and the bathroom. A claw-foot bathtub, no less. And chintz curtains to match the canopy bed."

Laura sat with legs outstretched. "I really am tired."

"Your day started early if you left the beach this morning and did all this running around tonight."

"Pastor Gregory—" She wasn't sure how to put it, but she wanted to ask a few questions about him.

"Reverend Gregory Hall is not what he appears," Ruth said as she poured a scant spoonful of sugar in her tea. "He's gruff, brusque, whatever adjective you want to use, but he's as good and kind as they come. You just have to get used to him."

"I love those boys already."

"Then you'll certainly do. Yes, you certainly will."

Laura wanted to ask more questions, but after two yawns, Ruth took the larger suitcase, saying, "Used to carrying these, so don't you worry a whit." Laura followed her up the stairs to a room on the left.

The bedroom was large and airy, painted in delicate yellow with a splash of orange. Laura loved it immediately. Tulips filled a vase on the vanity.

"I may never leave this room at all," she said, responding to Ruth's good-night hug.

Later, after slipping into nightclothes, she thought of the psalm she had memorized as a child in Sunday school. "Give thanks to the Lord, for he is good; his love endures forever."

The down comforter and pillows seemed to pull Laura in. As she sunk into their warm depths, she wondered what tomorrow would bring.

seven

Laura slept long and hard that first night in the bed-and-breakfast. The mountain air was soothing, so different from the dampness, fog, and wind at the beach. She liked it here. She had no idea how long she might stay, but for now she felt a thread of contentment stirring inside her. She'd buy and send postcards today and call Renee with the phone number. Nobody had missed her except Renee. She'd have to find another walking buddy.

Following a quick bath in the huge tub, she chose a lime green sweatshirt, blue denims, and her worn-in sneakers. After breakfast, she'd take a short walk through town, acquainting herself with her surroundings, then head to the church and her meeting with Reverend Hall. She was eager to see the church, the inside as well as out, and wondered about the piano. One day away from the keys and she was more than ready to play.

Laura's stomach growled as the smell of bacon floated up the stairs. Bacon and eggs. How long since she'd eaten an honest-to-goodness breakfast? It brought back pleasant memories of Saturday mornings when she and Jerry lingered over breakfast before planning their day. Sundays were filled with church and having brunch afterwards. She grabbed her coat and headed down.

Ruth bustled back and forth from table to stove. "I heard the water running, so I started putting together a good meal before you go look the job site over." She handed Laura a cup of coffee. "If you're like me, you need this to get going in the morning."

"Are you doing all this just for me?" Laura asked, looking at the eggs in the skillet. "You don't have anyone else staying over. Surely you didn't think you had to cook for me?"

"Sit, child." Ruth pointed. "I love cooking. I like having someone to cook for, so be prepared."

Child. Laura had to laugh. How long since anyone had called her *child?* In fact, she didn't think she'd ever been called it.

Ruth set a platter on the table. "Everybody should have a substantial breakfast. No little Continental meal here. Don't believe in them."

"If I don't watch out, I'll weigh two hundred pounds."

Ruth gave her a sideways glance. "You can skip lunch or dinner, but breakfast is a must."

Laura dug into the plate of food, pausing long enough to exclaim how delicious everything tasted.

"You know God works in mysterious ways," Ruth said. "You must believe that. Why else would you end up in Joseph? God sees someone's need, and clear across the state and north of that, a woman needs to get on with her life. I like the scripture from Daniel: 'There is a God in heaven who reveals mysteries.' "

"I don't deny that," Laura said with a nod. "I just hope I fit in."

"I think you already have." Ruth sat across from Laura. "Here. Eat more. There's a lot of food here."

Laura filled her plate again, surprised she was so hungry. At home a bowl of cereal sufficed. She also knew there was no way she'd win an argument with Ruth, at least not over eating the food she prepared. It was as Gregory had said: Ruth liked people. Their problems were her problems, and she was happiest when she was plying them with food.

"I'll help with the dishes," Laura offered, "then I'd better get over to the church."

"Scoot. Don't even think about it. If I get busy later on in the summer, you can clear the table, but I don't expect guests to help."

"I'm hardly a guest."

"To me you are."

Laura pushed her chair back. "Am I going to freeze out there? This is the heaviest coat I own."

"Mornings are cold this time of year. There's a jacket in the hall. I keep a supply of wraps for people who don't realize how cold it is up here in these mountains."

The coat was long, turquoise poplin with a warm flannel lining. "Wow!" Laura exclaimed. "I can play in the snow with this."

"You can still find snow up at the lake."

"I noticed that last night." She added mittens and a black knit hat that pulled down over her ears. "I feel ready for the North Pole."

"If you stick around, you'll get to see some dandy cold weather." Ruth handed her a package. "Some cookies to take to Pastor."

Laura stuck the wrapped package in one of the deep pockets. "I'm on my way."

"Don't get lost," Ruth called out.

Laura laughed at the thought. The church was but three blocks away. Joseph itself consisted of four, possibly five long blocks. There were no other main roads, just the one going through town and toward Wallowa Lake in a southerly direction and one going north and west to Enterprise.

Laura glanced up at the high school on the opposite hill. Several yellow buses were parked up next to the guardrail. She'd drive up there one day soon.

She walked briskly toward the first store. Her breath could be seen in the cold morning air. She took a deep breath and felt the icy cold fill her chest. Yes, this was different from beach living. People might think she was crazy for coming here when people longed to get away to vacation at the coast, but she was going to like it. Once again she felt confirmation that this was where she was needed, where God wanted her to be.

She thought of one of her favorite Scriptures, Psalm 16:11: "You have made known to me the path of life; you will fill me with joy in your presense, with eternal pleasures at your right hand."

The stone church sat like a welcoming beacon on a corner. Laura stood and looked at the old building. Steps led to the main door, and there was a side door alongside the street. It was old. It looked so different from the clapboard church back home.

She ran up the stairs and tried the front door. It opened. She stepped into a small foyer where people could hang their coats and shake off any mud or snow they might carry into the building. She took off the coat and left the hat and mittens on a hook. The cookies were an offering, a conversation starter, if nothing else.

The sanctuary was straight ahead. It was a "U" shape with the pulpit front and center and rows of seats to the left for a choir. Two aisles came to the center. The leaded glass windows on three sides lent a cheery atmosphere. Most importantly, a black piano sat to the left of the pulpit, right under the choir section. No organ, just a piano. It was beautiful, and she couldn't wait to play, but first things first.

"So, do you find our little church to your liking, so far?"

She whirled to find Gregory standing in an open doorway to the right.

"I like it very much." Her cheeks were flushed from her walk, but also from something else. "I hope I'm not too late. Here. Cookies from Ruth."

He nodded. "Something to go with my midmorning coffee break. Perhaps you'd like to join me in the kitchen? Or do you prefer the office?"

Laura shrugged. "Either is fine with me. But no cookies. I just ate one of Ruth's fantastic country farm breakfasts and doubt that I'll need to eat for the rest of the day."

Gregory held the door open, and she caught the scent of aftershave, a nice woodsy, pine smell.

The fellowship hall was large, with a kitchen against one wall and tables and chairs set up in orderly rows.

"This is a lovely church. You must be happy working here."

His eyes glazed over as he handed her a cup of steaming coffee. "I love the church. The area. The people."

"But something is missing?" The minute Laura said it, she wanted to bite her tongue. It was none of her business what lay behind the sometimes sad, lonely look in the deep blue eyes. He was like a chameleon, because now he was smiling.

"My sermons leave something to be desired, but the people stick with me."

"Do I hear a bit of negativity in your voice, Pastor?"

"Yes, that you do."

He finished the coffee and two of the peanut butter cookies while Laura had just one sip.

"I want to hear you play now, if you don't mind. We can talk after you play these hymns, which are scheduled to go with Sunday's message."

Laura wiped her hands and rose. "I've been itching to get at those keys." She smiled. Three of her favorites were listed. "Amazing Grace," one from her Sunday school playing days, "What a Friend We Have in Jesus" was another, and "Sweet, Sweet Spirit."

She went to the sanctuary, pulled the bench out, and held her fingers over the ivories. She'd first run through the scales. Sort of a warm-up like runners stretched before a marathon. This was a test and she wanted to do well.

After the second exercise of running up and down the keyboard, she was delighted that it was completely in tune. A voice called out, "Do we get to hear that every morning as the people come in, or is this your rendition of 'Amazing Grace'?"

Laura stopped playing. Was he being facetious or making fun of her? She wasn't sure.

"I always warm up, like an athlete," she said without turning around. She didn't have to look to see the brooding eyes.

"Whatever, it's beautiful," he said, turning back toward his office.

"Well!" Laura said aloud. "Looks like I've passed the first step."

She played the Gloria Patri, the Doxology, and her favorite seven-chord Amen response. She still hadn't played the hymns, but now everything came out of her, songs she didn't need music for. Songs that uplifted her soul, made her realize how much a part of her life God was. "The Lord's Prayer," "The Old Rugged Cross," "How Great Thou Art," and Charles Wesley's "O For a Thousand Tongues to Sing."

A clapping interrupted the end of the song. She turned to find Pastor Gregory Michael Hall applauding.

"No book? You know all of these from memory?"

Laura stood and bowed. "Yes. I've been playing for the past forty years. How could I not memorize them?"

"Astounding."

"Now I will play the required hymns."

"In what key?"

"Which key do you prefer?"

Gregory raised his hands in resignation. "Whichever you choose."

Laura played another hour, loving the piano, the sound as it filled the church. What a gift this was, to play again in honor of her Lord Jesus Christ.

She closed the lid reluctantly and headed to the office.

Looking up, Gregory motioned her to the chair across from him. "I couldn't be more happy with your playing," he said.

"In fact," he closed the book, "would you possibly consider giving Caleb lessons?"

"Caleb?" Somehow she couldn't imagine his wanting to play the piano. "I would think Caleb would choose a band instrument. If not a horn, perhaps a clarinet or something else in the woodwind family."

Gregory leaned forward. "His mother was a pianist, and he's taken it as a fancy to learn. Insists on it. That's been a year or so ago, but there are no teachers here in Joseph."

"Well, I taught my own children, or the two that wanted to learn."

"So you would be an answer to prayer. Make that two prayers."

"Would there be others who might like lessons?" Laura had often thought of teaching in Sealand, but there were two other teachers. By the time her children were raised, there were no openings.

"I'm sure there would be."

"Did your wife play for the church?"

"Yes, and though she was accomplished, she didn't take to it as you did. Never felt she was quite good enough to play for an audience."

Laura looked at a photo on the file cabinet. "I assume this is her?"

Gregory handed it over. "Yes. Taken just before she had Caleb."

A young woman smiled back at her. Love shone in her eyes, giving her a look of radiance and happiness. Was it the loss of her that made Gregory such a quiet, reflective person?

"Very nice." Laura noticed school photos of both sons. Joel definitely had his father's good looks, the same brooding eyes. "I'd be happy to give Caleb lessons if he can work it in between his baseball practice and school homework."

"He will. Caleb can do anything he sets his mind to."

"And Joel?"

"Quite the opposite. He could do it, but he doesn't have the confidence to try."

"Perhaps he needs to be encouraged."

His eyes narrowed. "And you think I don't encourage him?"

"I didn't say that."

"You didn't need to." Gregory leaned over and picked up Caleb's photo, as if to change the subject. "Caleb's like his mother in many ways. He would very much like for me to find a mother for him, but, to be perfectly honest, I have no desire to marry again. Just thought you'd want to know that."

Laura's cheeks flushed for the second time that morning. "Well, I suppose it would be good to let you know I have no intention of marrying again, either. There is no one that could possibly replace my husband, Jerry."

She stood and moved toward the door. Gregory stood also. "Look, I didn't mean to—"

Laura laughed, but it sounded hollow. Could she work for this man? Did she even want to? "It's all right. I believe in being aboveboard with things like that. I'm glad you set the record straight."

The wind had calmed down and the sun shone out of a clear blue sky, but Laura did not want to walk now. All she wanted was to go back to Ruth's and bury her head in the pillow on the comfortable bed. How she missed Jerry. How she missed having someone to bare her soul to. How she missed that special part of belonging to someone, of being one in God. She knew she'd never find another partner who loved God as she did or knew things about her. That's why she would stay single. But it still hurt. From deep within, a longing challenged her, like a haunting melody.

eight

Ruth was dusting the sitting room with a long-handled feather duster when Laura banged in the front door. She hadn't meant to close the door so hard. Ruth glanced around the corner.

"Hello, honey. How'd it go?"

She shrugged out of the mittens, hat, and coat. "My playing passed inspection."

"But?"

"My personality obviously doesn't."

"Oh, my, my." Ruth set the duster down. "Sounds like it's time to put the teakettle on. I was about ready to have some lunch anyway."

"Nothing for me, please. I just want to go upstairs and try to figure out why I thought I should do this."

Ruth came over and put her arm around Laura. "I take it Gregory put his foot in his mouth again. He's quite good at it, you know."

Laura squared her shoulders. "Contrary to what Reverend Hall thinks, I did not come to Joseph to find a husband! I do not want a husband! I do not need a husband!"

"Calm down, dear." Ruth's blue eyes twinkled ever so slightly. "I happen to know if God wants you to have a man in your life again, He'll point the way and I doubt that you'll refuse."

"It had better be pretty clear." Laura tried to relax. "He wants me to give Caleb lessons. Says I play magnificently. Couldn't believe I didn't need the hymnal."

"You don't?"

"Heavens, no. I've been playing all those hymns since I can remember."

"Well, I am impressed now. I was wishing we had a piano here for you to practice on, but sounds as if you don't need to practice anyway."

"One always needs to practice."

"Just as one needs to read the Bible, even if it's been read through before."

"Exactly. I don't want to talk about this just now. I need some time and some space."

"You sure you don't want a cup of my famous potato corn chowder?"

"Not yet. My stomach's in knots."

"It'll just take a minute to heat up whenever you come down."

Laura climbed the stairs and entered the beautifully decorated room. She fell across the bed and let the tears come. What did she want? What did she need? Was this a good step? Was God directing her? If so, why did she feel this pain and rejection? Or was she overreacting?

Jerry used to tell her, "You go to the extremes, honey. You have a problem, say with one of the kids, and rather than try to figure a simple solution, you imagine the worst possible result. That's being awfully negative." Had she been negative when she feared that he might not come back from fishing one day? *What about that, God? You took him from me and I wasn't ready to let go.*

Laura remembered the verse Jerry used to recite to her, James 1:6: "But when he asks, he must believe and not doubt, because he who doubts is like a wave of the sea, blown and tossed by the wind." How like Jerry to find the perfect verse to taunt her with. But God had taken Jerry; and though she was not supposed to question God or wonder, she couldn't help it at times. Right now she missed Renee and her comfort, her wisdom.

Laura drifted off to sleep and woke when the doorbell sounded.

Ruth's voice floated up the stairs as Laura rose, straightened her clothes, and ran a brush through her hair. Her eyes still had dark smudges below. It was a male voice. Probably Gregory, yet it didn't sound like him. Maybe someone needed a room for the night.

Footsteps sounded on the stairs, then a light tap. "Laura? There's someone here to see you. From the paper."

Laura groaned.

"You okay? Still napping?"

She added a touch of lipstick and glanced in the oval gilt-edged mirror. Her eyes didn't have their usual sparkle. She wondered if they had when she flounced out of the pastor's office. She finally descended the stairs.

"Ms. Madison?" A young man with long hair past his shirt collar stepped forward, holding out a hand. "I'm Eddie from the *Chieftain*. I probably should have called first, but I was in the area. I understand you're going to be the pianist for the Community Church."

"Yes, but—"

"You placed an ad in our paper and got results. That's part of the coverage, but I also want to interview you—do a feature for our paper. Can we sit at the table, Ruth?"

"Of course." She indicated the round table in the sitting room. "I'll bring something to drink."

Laura wasn't ready for this. She saw the camera and flash equipment in the young man's case. "I can't do this now."

Ruth came over. "She's had a busy day so far, Eddie. Maybe you could come back in a day or so?"

"Well, sure. But it won't take long. I'll just take a couple of shots and a bit of info—"

Ruth spoke up for Laura. "That's the problem. She isn't ready for a photo. A lady needs time to prepare herself."

Eddie nodded, closing his notebook. "I understand. Sorry I didn't call first."

"You might come to hear her play on Sunday," Ruth suggested, handing him a cup and offering a plate of cookies. "That way you could really get a good story."

Laura had to smile. Ruth was cagey. It was a good way to get the young man into church. "I'd love to talk to you the first of next week," she offered.

"Of course." He spoke with a cookie in his mouth.

"Actually, dear, he came by for some of my peanut butter cookies." She winked. "He knows I bake them on Wednesdays."

"Oh, Ruth," they said in unison.

"You can stay for dinner, if you'd like."

Eddie downed his coffee and jumped to his feet. "Thanks, but I'll take a rain check on that."

"I appreciate your speaking up for me," Laura said once the reporter was gone, and she sunk back into the cushions of the settee. "I just couldn't face something like that right now."

"I know. That's why I ran—what do they call it in football? —interference."

"Yeah, something like that."

"Do you feel better?" Ruth leaned over, brushing the hair back from Laura's face. "You still look a mite peaked to me."

"I think it might take another day to get back to normal. If there is such a thing."

"At least you have two days before Sunday."

"When I'll be under scrutiny."

"If you were interested in someone, I have just the person," Ruth said then. "Our most confirmed bachelor has let it be known—in fact, put it on the prayer chain—that he'd very much like to find a wife."

"Oh, Ruth. I really am not looking for that sort of thing."

"You could do worse than Kenny Thompson."

"I'll be so busy playing and giving lessons that I won't

miss there not being someone in my life."

"Perhaps so, perhaps so," Ruth said, dusting the shelf behind Laura's head. "Still, you can't blame me for being a romantic at heart."

Laura grabbed the crocheting out of a bag she'd brought. She was making scarves out of a nice navy blue wool. "No, I guess not."

❧

Gregory watched Laura retreat from his office. He felt like such a—what was it the boys called it?—a doofus. Why had he said that, intimating Laura had come to Joseph looking for a husband? She was probably just as content to be single as he was and had been for the past eight, almost nine years.

He picked up the photo of Shirley, warming at the smile. She had been a wonderful woman, a God-fearing woman, and the one he thought God had selected for him after his engagement to Beth Marie fell through. That had been so many years ago now.

He had a faded snapshot of himself and Beth at the county fair in his wallet. That had been a happy time. Yet wasn't first love the most poignant, the most deeply felt, the most intense? He had never quite forgotten her, though he had been a good and dutiful husband to Shirley.

He put the picture back, his mind going to another smile, a warm smile, indicating an easygoing nature. He didn't know Laura Madison that well, but she had gotten to him, making her way into a tiny corner of his heart in a way no one had since Shirley died. How ridiculous, since he had barely met her. Something about her piano playing, the way her hands flew over the ivories made him realize here was a woman of God. She played flawlessly, but it was the delivery, the way she put her feeling and her heart into it. He had been moved wholeheartedly. God had sent her to this small church in Joseph, Oregon, when she could have played anywhere. He had not known her long, but in those few hours she had been positive and encouraging about Joel, thinking he could play a solo for a future church service. He knew Joel would never do it, but she had seemed so confident. And Caleb, bless his exuberant self, had taken to her instantly. Gregory believed in divine intervention. He'd always said, "What was meant to be was meant to be."

So what had made him say such a thing to Laura? Why did he blunder like this? Why could he get along with most people, but when it came to relationships with women, he was in left field? Maybe she would change her mind now. He wouldn't blame her if she did.

The door opened and Caleb stuck his head around the corner. "Dad?"

"Come on in, Son."

"Is Laura here?"

"No. Did you think she would be?"

The boy slumped into the nearest chair. "I just thought she might have come by to practice the piano."

Gregory leaned forward. "I'll tell you one thing. No, make that two things. And both should make you happy."

"What's that, Dad? Say, do you have any cookies or anything around? I'm starved!"

Gregory produced the last two peanut butter cookies. "Here. Just for you. Guess who made them?"

"Ruth," Caleb said, crumbs falling out of his mouth. "But what's the big news?"

"Mrs. Madison is an accomplished pianist. I enjoyed hearing her play for an hour or better this morning."

"And?"

"She's willing to give you lessons if you still want them."

"Really? Are you making this up, Dad?"

"No. Would I make something like that up? I asked and she said she'd love to."

"She likes me."

"How can you be so sure?"

He wrinkled his nose. "She just does. A guy can tell."

Gregory felt a jolt to his midsection. Maybe that's what bothered him. There had been a magnetism. Laura, unlike him, showed her emotions by her facial expressions. He knew she felt something for him, and it was this fact that made him feel something. A tiny flutter, but still it was something. *No, it couldn't be.*

"I think Laura was happy to go to your game and enjoyed you, all right. She has two boys, you know."

"I can't wait to start lessons. When can I? Huh, Dad?"

"One question at a time, Caleb. How many times do I have to tell you that?" He leaned over and ruffled Caleb's hair. "About time for a haircut, I think."

"When can I start, Dad?"

"Whenever you want, I imagine. After Sunday, that is."

"I say Monday right after baseball practice then."

"You'd better check with her before you make any big plans. See what a good time is for her."

"Oh, Dad! I can't believe it! In one day we have a piano player and I'm going to take piano lessons. Now I can play piano just like my mother did."

Gregory winced. "That you can, Caleb. Yes, that you can."

The boy raced out of his office and whooped all the way down the block. He was probably heading over to Ruth's. He closed his book and shut his eyes. No sense in trying to concentrate anymore today. He'd tackle his sermon topic first thing in the morning, though he liked to have it ready by Thursday. He still had the bulletin to prepare. Well, tomorrow was another day.

nine

Laura realized after that first Sunday that she needed to shop for a new dress or suit. A dressy jacket, a skirt or two, a scarf, and a strand of pearls. She might order from a catalogue. She'd thought it would be more casual dress, like the beach, but the women in the little community church dressed up and obviously had their hair done on Saturdays.

Ruth had prayed with her that first morning. "Remember what Matthew says: 'Surely I am with you always.' "

"I know. I think of that Scripture a lot."

Laura met with Gregory thirty minutes before the service to go over the special music. He looked expectant as she quietly entered his office. It was different from the other day when she'd flounced out, and she really hoped he wouldn't bring that matter up. Caleb had wheeled over to Ruth's all excited at the prospect of taking lessons. His first lesson was the next day. He didn't want to waste time.

"Thanks for giving Caleb the time he wanted for his first lesson."

"I have no schedule other than Sunday morning and night and any other special wedding or funeral service."

"Yes, ah, well."

Laura looked into his eyes and immediately glanced away. There was something there she could not read, and it bothered her.

"I had hoped you could play a fifteen-minute prelude before the service instead of the usual ten."

"That's fine."

"You know everyone has been champing at the bit, wanting

to see the new pianist."

She had to smile. "This is my big debut."

"You'll pass with flying colors; I have no doubt about that."

"Pastor?" An elderly gentleman tapped on the door as he entered. "I—oh, hello. You must be Mrs. Madison."

"Laura. Please."

"We're so happy to have you. I'm Tom Cantrell."

"I'll be with you in a second, Tom."

"I think I have a piano to go play," Laura said, moving past the gentleman. She was glad she'd brought the black-and-white houndstooth jacket, her best outfit. Laura felt two pairs of eyes on her as she left the room.

She started playing, adding extra chords as the people came in. The only ones she could see without turning were to her left, and those pews filled up fast. New members, she surmised. A murmur of voices soon filled the church. A few people, she figured, were partially deaf, because they spoke loud enough for Laura to hear above her piano playing.

"She's nice-looking!"

"And younger than we thought!"

"Plays better than Gert or Amanda."

"Especially Amanda. Poor little dear really tried, too."

Caleb bounced up, greeting Laura warmly. "I hope I can learn to play even half that good!" His eyes snapped with enthusiasm.

"You will," she whispered, leaning over for a brief second.

He frowned. "How can you play and talk to me at the same time?"

"Because I've been playing many, many years."

"I better go sit down or Dad will get mad at me."

"See you later."

"We're having chocolate cake and white cake and it's all decorated up special for you and the new members," he said.

Laura grinned. "Were you supposed to tell me?"

"Oops!" He covered his mouth. "Maybe not."

Laura looked at her watch. Two minutes and Gregory would come in. When he started walking down the aisle, she changed the tempo to something slow and soft. He caught her eye minutes later, and she stopped playing.

When she played for the singing, she realized how good it was to hear voices again. She never missed a cue as she went through the hymns, following a tall, serious-faced lady who led the singing. She wondered about a choir. She'd have to ask Ruth if they had one.

Gregory chose to introduce her before the announcements. "God has answered many prayers by bringing Mrs. Laura Madison into our midst, and I know you'll enjoy her playing as much as I have already." He beamed at her.

Laura stood and bowed slightly. This was the part she didn't like. She looked out at the congregation, smiling at Caleb, who clapped harder than anyone else did. Joel sat in the back, a frown on his young face. *Does he ever smile?* she couldn't help wondering.

"Laura often plays without the hymnal," Gregory added. "Believe me when I tell you she is accomplished and will bring much happiness and singing to our little church. It's also a special Sunday for another reason, as we'll be welcoming new members."

❧

The singing went fast, and Laura felt happy as she listened to the voices, some loud, some off-key. She sang as she played, as she always had.

" 'Forgiveness' is my text this morning," Gregory began his sermon. "All of us have done something or said something we're sorry for. It is my hope that the one who was offended would be forgiving."

Laura felt color rise in her cheeks. Had he changed his sermon since the day she'd been in the office? She doubted it.

The service ended, the new members joined, and the last song was sung.

"My dear, we are so happy to have you," one after another said, stopping by the piano as she played the postlude following the benediction.

"Thank you, thank you," she repeated.

"You are coming to our special coffee hour," more than one said.

Then Ruth came. "My dear, I am absolutely enthralled at your playing. I'd come to hear you even if I was a heathen."

Laura laughed and stood to hug the older woman. "Do you think I passed muster?"

"Oh, my goodness, everyone is raving about the music. Caleb is very fortunate to have you as a teacher."

Laura knew she'd never remember the names, but she'd remember Clyde, the man who stood over everyone else, and Miriam, who poured coffee and exclaimed over the piano playing. It was good to be needed. She hoped Gregory was happy with the morning's music as well.

"Don't eat too much cake," Caleb said, coming up to her side. "We'll be going over to Ruth's for brunch, you know."

"You are?"

"We always do."

"Oh." She scraped the icing off the cake, then felt guilty for doing so.

"We'll see you tonight," voices called out as she headed for the room where her coat hung.

"Now, Ruth, you sure you want us to come today?" It was Gregory asking about brunch.

"And why would you not come today?"

"Well, it's too much."

"Dad, we gotta go! Besides, I have to discuss my lesson with Laura."

Laura slipped back into the other room. So Gregory was

trying to get out of going to Ruth's. It had to do with her. That was fine. He didn't have to like her or she him. She had a job to do, and do it she would.

Since she was wearing her good clothes, Laura had driven to church. She went out the door while the others continued with their coffee and cake. She'd get back to Ruth's and slip into something more casual and comfortable. Thank heavens for Caleb. If he were like his father or older brother, it would be pretty dismal.

Her stomach growled at the smell of a baking ham. She'd had a slice of toast for breakfast and that had been early. Ruth had also baked a rhubarb custard pie, everyone's favorite. "I do hope you like rhubarb."

"That I do," Laura assured her.

"Good. Rhubarb is something you either like or you don't."

Laura wore a pair of brown corduroy slacks and a turquoise heavy knit sweater. After combing her hair, she hurried down to see if she could help set the table. The Halls had just arrived.

"Laura! I looked everywhere for you." Caleb's eager face looked up as she came down the steps.

"So, you're ready for your lesson?"

"You bet."

"Kenny Thompson, the gentleman I mentioned to you, was looking for you, too," Ruth said. "I rather imagine he'll be calling you sometime this week."

Laura shook her head. "I'm not interested, Ruth. Surely you told him that."

"It wouldn't hurt to go have coffee with him," Ruth said.

"He's a bachelor, has land. Lots of it," Gregory added. "Almost married back in the sixties, but his fiancée died in a car accident and he just never dated again. Not that he doesn't want to marry, because he told me that he did."

"Asked to have his request on the prayer chain," Ruth added.

"I say let's eat," Laura said. Anything to get the subject off of her dating.

"I agree," Caleb said. "I'm starving."

"This is your favorite meal," Ruth said as she brought the potatoes and ham out. "And a pie for dessert."

They held hands while Gregory asked the blessing.

After they ate, Caleb asked, "Is the pie rhubarb?"

"I bet it is," Gregory said.

Joel said nothing.

"You'll see," Ruth said with a wink.

Laura laughed when the boys banged their forks on the table.

"We want pie!" Caleb proclaimed.

"We like pie!" Joel joined in.

"We love rhubarb!" Gregory added.

"And I do, too," Laura said.

"Okay, okay," Ruth said good-naturedly. "Yes, it's rhubarb and there's enough for a big slice for all."

Gregory winked at Ruth. "She spoils us all—"

"And loves doing it," Laura said. She'd gotten up to get the dessert plates and forks. Ruth insisted that no one need lick his or her forks around her table. There were always clean ones for dessert.

"You don't like rhubarb," Ruth said, watching Laura's fork in midair.

"Oh, no, but I do. I'm savoring every bite."

The boys dug into their pie, seemingly oblivious to the adult conversation. Laura took one bite and just held it in her mouth. She hadn't had rhubarb custard pie since her mother baked it when she was a girl. It was just as good as she remembered.

After dinner, Caleb pushed his chair back. "Please, may I be excused and can I go skateboarding?"

Gregory shrugged. "This is the way it goes. Every week.

Caleb can't wait to use the skateboard."

Joel excused himself and went to the gold room to read.

Laura fetched the coffeepot. One more cup would go good.

After Ruth cleared the table, she brought out the Scrabble game. "I didn't tell you this part, but we play at least one game before Gregory heads for home."

"Scrabble! But I love to play and haven't for ages."

Gregory smiled. "Uh-oh. Something tells me we've met our match."

"Doesn't Joel want to play?" Laura asked. It was one game all three of her children enjoyed. Jerry hadn't, but always joked about the fierce competition the four of them had on Saturday nights. The games stopped when Kurt left for college.

"Joel always reads," Ruth said.

"Did you ask him to play?" Laura asked.

"Probably, a long time ago."

"I'll ask him now," Laura said.

He scowled when she entered the room after first tapping on the door. "We're playing Scrabble and I thought you might like to play."

"I never play."

"Because you don't want to? Or why not?"

He shrugged. There was a lonely look on his face and an intensity that bothered Laura. He needed to talk to someone, and obviously it couldn't be his father.

"I'd like you to be my partner."

He followed her down the hall.

"We're playing partners."

"We never played that way," Ruth said.

"Well, it's simple. You just combine our scores, just as you do yours and Pastor's."

"Sure, why not?" Ruth changed the page for scoring. "I'm always game to try something new."

"I think it's a good idea," Gregory said with a nod.

Joel said nothing, but his face brightened when he drew an "A," which meant he had first turn. "Hey, that was a lucky draw."

"You still have to make the letters fit," Laura added quickly. When Joel wrote "quilt" and received forty-eight points, he beamed.

Laura and Joel won the game, as she had figured they would. She knew Joel would be good with words, just as he was with numbers, and playing his trumpet, and anything else he set his mind to.

When Caleb ran in, he was surprised to see the game already over and even more surprised to see Joel was playing.

"Hey, man, way cool," he said when he noticed Joel and Laura had won by twenty-five points. "That's great. Maybe I should learn to play, too."

"Yes, I think you should," Ruth said. "I won't always be able to play once the tourist season starts."

Laura helped clear up the game and watched while the three left. If she wasn't mistaken, Joel's head was just a bit higher than usual.

ten

Laura enjoyed the evening service because it was less formal. After everyone left, she could hardly wait to get back to Ruth's to relax. She had lots of things to mull over. She thought about Kenny Thompson, deciding it wouldn't hurt to go out for coffee, should he ask.

He asked the following morning.

The voice was deep, yet gruff. She wondered if he'd found it as difficult to call her as she was finding it difficult to talk now.

"Mrs. Madison, I'll be in town, doing some banking. Maybe we could meet at the café for lunch?"

Glancing over her shoulder, she knew Ruth was halfway listening.

"I—well, I have a piano lesson at four."

"Oh, hey, I gotta be back at the ranch long before that."

"Okay. Noon sounds fine."

"He's a good man," Ruth said, after Laura had hung up. "You'd never have to worry about money again or need to play the piano. I imagine the only thing his wife would need to do is learn to ride a horse and maybe lasso one."

Laura laughed. "I suppose he would want someone to ride with him on that big spread. I'm not sure I like horses. Never been on one, if you can believe that."

"That can change with a few riding lessons."

"I'm just not interested, Ruth. Give it up."

"It's just lunch."

❧

Laura was laying out her music lessons, glad she'd packed a

beginner's book. Caleb would take to the lessons quickly. He didn't have a piano to practice on at home, but his father said he was looking for a good used one. She had changed into warm tweed slacks, a pair that had been in her wardrobe forever because she never threw things out, when the phone rang.

Ruth's voice called out at the door. "Laura? May I come in?"

"Of course." She set the hairbrush down and motioned for Ruth to sit in the one vacant chair. The bed was dotted with discarded clothes, the music books, her diary, and her Bible.

Ruth chuckled. "You use the bed like I do. Lay it all out."

"Yes, makes it easier. Was the phone for me?"

"Yes. It was Kenny Thompson. Seems he has a dying calf and must make a run to the vet's instead of coming into Joseph to go to the bank. Said he knew you'd understand."

Laura glanced upward. "Thank You, Lord, because I wasn't ready for this lunch."

Ruth patted her arm. "I am glad you aren't upset—"

"Upset? Ruth, how could I be? I know what cattle mean to people who ranch for a living."

After Ruth went back downstairs, Laura wrote Renee a letter, dropped off a line to Kurt and to Jen, and sent Jeff a note at his last known address. She wrote another letter and enclosed one of the photos of her new church to her old one. They'd post it on the bulletin board to let everyone know how she was faring.

At three she walked over to the church.

Caleb was a fast learner. Laura thought he would be. He operated under the theory that he could do anything he set his mind to. Again, she wished Joel had that same confidence.

"You may want to be out on the ball field or shooting baskets," Laura said that first afternoon, "but playing the piano is something you'll have with you all of your life. I don't ask for long practices. Thirty minutes a day is fine. We'll start with scales."

Caleb looked apprehensive. "Scales?"

"Yes, like this." Laura made him stand so she would have plenty of elbowroom as she placed her fingers over the keys. She remembered dreading the scales when she first started piano lessons, but she wondered why now. She explained the treble clef and bass clef, showing Caleb how to hold his fingers poised over the keys.

"Soon you'll have the keys memorized, and later, if you like, we can play duets. You can play the right hand while I play the left or vice versa."

"Hey, way cool! I'd like that." His eyes were shining. "Maybe we can play for church."

Laura nodded. "We'll start at an evening service. People tend to be more relaxed and forgive mistakes."

"You never make mistakes."

Laura laughed. "Oh, yes, I do. You just don't hear them, as I cover them up quick." She rose, motioning for Caleb to sit back down.

"Do you really think I can learn to play good enough for church?"

"Of course. But first things first. We'll learn about flats and sharps and timing. Timing is very important. I'm going to estimate you need two years of practice first."

"Two years? Really?" Being a kid, he was used to instant gratification, and the thought of taking two years seemed almost insurmountable.

"Practice makes perfect. Just like baseball, painting a picture, or, you name it."

Caleb nodded. "Guess I never thought of it that way."

"So, are you ready to begin?"

"Sure."

"Scales are a good warm-up, and you know about warmups." She leaned over the piano. "Like this." Music filled the small church. "Of course, you'll have a book. I've brought one about scales and one for beginners. I'll expect you to do one set of scales a week."

Caleb's fingers flew up and down the keyboard, playing nothing in particular. *He has a natural flair, a good touch for it,* Laura thought. But he would. Of course he would, because that's the way he was.

"The only thing I don't like about the piano is you can't play in the band."

Laura nodded. "This is true. Would you rather play a horn or drum or something you can play in a band?"

"Nah. If I'm playing a sport, I can't be in the band, too. Besides, Dad agrees I should learn piano because my mother knew how to play and he says he likes piano."

"You don't have a piano now," Laura said. "Did you ever have one?"

Caleb shrugged. "I think so, but Dad says we lived in a tiny house when I was born and my mother sold her piano."

"Oh, I do hope she didn't sell her very own piano."

Caleb shrugged again. "You can ask my dad. He can tell you. I don't know anything about my mother."

"From what I hear, she was a fine woman and loved you very, very much."

"I know."

Laura opened the beginning music book and started with basic key knowledge. "We always being with middle C." She placed his thumb on the key.

The lesson flew by. Laura could scarcely believe it was already five.

"You can come to church to practice every day. I think it best if you use the old upright in the fellowship hall, though I want to use this one for the lessons."

"Dad will get me a piano," Caleb said.

"Yes. He said he was checking ads for a good used one. Ruth is looking also. Says she's always wanted one for what she calls the music room. So, that's enough for today. Follow my instructions. I wrote them down on this page taped to the back. That way you won't lose it and can't say, 'Oh, I forgot.' "

"I won't forget, Laura."

"Well, you just might. Practice those scales every day, even though you may tire of them." She leaned over and ruffled his hair. He turned and impulsively hugged her.

"Thanks, Laura." Then he bounced up the aisle, holding his two music books close, as if they were treasures. He paused at the doorway and turned to wave. "I hope I do well this week."

"You will, Caleb. I know you will."

Laura half-expected Gregory to come out of his office to make some comments about the lesson, but he didn't appear. Since she needed to practice a new hymn, she sat playing for a few minutes. She seemed to lose all track of time when she was playing. It had always been that way.

A voice interrupted her playing.

"Mrs. Madison?"

Laura turned to find Joel standing there, his head bent.

"Joel, hello. What brings you here?"

"I came over after I finished my homework."

"Yes?"

He shifted from one foot to the other. "Been thinkin' about what you said. About the trumpet solo."

"And you want to play for church?" There was something about this child that made her want to reach out and pull him close. All he needed was a hug, a continual acceptance of who he was, what he could be if only he would try. He had a father, but he needed a mother's tenderness. Some children get by without a mother, but Joel had not fared well. Now there seemed to be this rift between him and his father.

"I'd love to work with you on that. Anytime you're ready."

"Do you think I could really do it?"

Her hand reached out and clasped his arm. "I don't think. I

know you can, Joel. I've never been more sure of anything."

He shifted his feet again, but said nothing.

She opened the hymnal. "I've been thinking of Father's Day. We use special music as we honor our fathers. Here, you can see here where the solo parts are." He leaned over. "Here at the beginning." She played it on the piano. "Then at the end of that first stanza, at the end of the second and third stanzas. It's quite effective. The trumpet is the only instrument that can bring this piece to life. It's glorious. I've heard it more than once and it gives me chills every time."

He mumbled. "Would I have to stand up here?"

"Yes, that's what I'd prefer."

"I'll think about it." He turned to go.

"There's plenty of time for practicing. I'll go with your schedule," Laura called after him.

He left the church, head bent again. Laura gathered her books and coat. She could hardly believe Joel had come in on his own. Had his father coached him? Somehow she doubted it.

The aroma of beef stew was in the air when Laura got home.

"It smells heavenly," she said, shrugging off her jacket.

"How did the lesson go?"

"Caleb's a natural," Laura replied. "I don't think there is anything Caleb couldn't do well. He just flows into anything he tries."

"Unlike Joel?" Ruth said.

"That's the neat thing, though."

"Neat?"

"Yes. Joel came. He says he'll practice the solo I mentioned earlier."

"No kidding." Ruth handed over a cup of coffee. "Dinner's about ready, but looks as if you could use this."

"Amen to that." She pulled up a chair. "One is never supposed to compare children, though we so often do. Joel's the eldest, and that usually offers some advantage, but not here. Not in this family."

"Look at Esau," Ruth said. "He was the eldest, but Jacob was the one that God found favor in."

"I believe God finds favor in all of His children," Laura said. "I have never thoroughly understood that story."

"Food was more important than anything else to Esau," Ruth said.

"But Jacob was cunning."

"And Caleb isn't cunning."

"Not in the slightest way. He loves and looks up to his brother. I wish I could see that Joel felt the same, but envy is written all over his face, and it shows in his actions. Caleb is obviously a thorn in his side."

"It's difficult for a boy to grow up without a mother," Ruth said. "Mothers sense problems long before most fathers do. My theory is that Caleb does so well because he never knew his mother. Joel, on the other hand, has memories and knows what it's like to experience a mother's love and understanding."

Laura nodded. "I was the buffer between Kurt and his father," Laura offered. "Smoothed things over more than one time."

"Do you want to eat now, or when?"

Laura hadn't even thought about food until she had gotten home, and she had to admit the smell was tantalizing. Of course, everything Ruth cooked was delicious. "I think I need to eat now, then get busy on some lesson plans for the Hall boys." She smiled and leaned back. She still couldn't believe that Joel had come in voluntarily. It was a good sign.

eleven

It was May, and Laura had been in Joseph a month. She and Ruth were in the sitting room while Ruth stitched an edging on new place mats and Laura wrote letters.

"I'm getting things done now, because once summer hits, I'll be so busy I won't have time to sit like this," remarked Ruth.

It was the first night they hadn't had a fire in the fireplace. Laura missed the crackling sound and the glow that had relaxed her while keeping her warm.

"You've sure made a difference in the short time you've been here," Ruth said, glancing up. "Some people are like that, you know."

"And you?" Laura set her pen down. "I suppose you think you don't affect everyone you know around here?"

"Well, I don't have any enemies that I know of." She bent back over her work. "We need to go to Enterprise to shop soon."

"I'd love to take you there."

"Good. Now I'm heading for bed." Ruth folded the material. "For some reason I seem to be more tired than usual."

"Yes," Laura said with a smile, "lots happened today."

She watched the kind lady amble out the door. Ruth slept in the small room, which had once been a nursery, at the end of the hall. Laura had no intentions of going to bed this early. She always had been a night owl. Besides, she had some mulling over to do. Her thoughts went back to her husband and children, and Joel and Caleb.

Though Jerry had been a wonderful father, a kind, supportive husband, he had had little patience with his eldest son.

Joel, like Kurt, had things to work out. Could Laura help boost his sagging confidence? If so, could she do it without stepping on the Reverend Gregory Hall's toes? More importantly, would he listen to Laura, who was really an outsider? She knew she wouldn't know unless she tried, and she had to try. She just did.

She set her letter aside and turned off the Tiffany lamp. She liked sitting in the darkness, enjoying the quiet. It was a pleasant room with a window bench on the south wall and a row of windows facing east to the mountains. The peaks were huge, outlined shadows against the dark sky. Tonight there was no wind, so the large sitting room seemed much warmer. Thick, long, wine-colored drapes hung from ceiling to floor. Before she went to bed, Ruth usually drew them, but not when Laura was still up. Laura would close them just before climbing the stairs to bed.

"Jerry," she murmured into the growing darkness. "I wish you were here with me, sharing this moment. I miss you so."

The hurt tore at her like a claw, and she fought back the threat of tears. Nights were bad back in Sealand, too. Nights were when they'd shared their day, sometimes read side by side, not interrupting, yet being together. Sometimes they played cribbage, Jerry's favorite game. On occasion they'd watched a video or a TV program. They had been comfortable together. She'd have to ask Ruth if that had bothered her after she was widowed. It had been twenty years, she'd told Laura. Perhaps she wouldn't even remember what it had been like, but then again, perhaps she would. She had a great memory.

Laura's Bible was on her stack of belongings. Its pungent leather was another memory of Jerry and how they'd often read Scripture together. He'd given her this Bible the Easter before he died. "I'm tired of seeing you read from a Bible that's falling apart," he'd said with a laugh.

"You always know what I need the most."

They'd embraced and she felt the beating of his heart against her body. They didn't make love, though she saw desire in his eyes. Why hadn't they? Was it because they were older and let the moment slip by? She didn't know, but often regretted that she hadn't been more spontaneous. If only she'd reached out to him that night, two nights before the boating accident. Now all she had were the memories of those good times, the times of closeness.

Laura's thoughts drifted to Gregory, and she wondered if he missed his wife, if he missed tender moments of passion. Somehow she didn't think they'd been as close a couple as she and Jerry had been. On occasion his eyes revealed a deep inner hurt, but it wasn't a pain like one felt over a loss. There was a problem, a much larger one, that Gregory carried deep inside him. She doubted he'd ever divulge anything, but in the event he did, she was a good listener. Laura had always prided herself on caring about people and being able to just listen and not offer advice.

She leaned back against the comfortable chair, pulling an ottoman over. She turned the light back on. Her Bible opened automatically to Philippians.

"I can do everything through him who gives me strength."

The verse had been Laura's mainstay. When things weren't going well, she clung to that verse and its wonderful, helpful meaning.

She read a few psalms because they uplifted her, then prayed in the darkness. For some reason her thoughts again returned to Gregory and his sermons. His preaching was calm, almost a monotone. Not that he had to preach fire and brimstone, but he could use a bit of inflection. Sometimes she wished she could stay at the piano while he preached instead of going into the audience at the first pew, right where she was in his line of view.

"Give it some oomph," she said aloud. "Make the Word

come to life, Gregory. Make the words zing with fervor!"

She wondered what it might be like to be a preacher. It took a special person to answer the calling. She'd never had the desire to be a missionary, though she knew several who had answered the mission call. There were other ways to serve God, and she was doing one of them.

かな

Gregory wasn't sure when he'd first started thinking about Laura in a way other than a friend, a parishioner. There was just something about her smile, the way she brushed her hair off her forehead. It was a nervous gesture, but an endearing one. He also liked how she related to the boys, encouraging them to do well. It had made a difference with Joel.

And she walked with head held high, with such confidence that one couldn't help noticing. Kenny Thompson had his eye on her. Kenny would be good for Laura, and they'd make a nice couple. He liked the idea, but on the other hand couldn't help feeling a twinge of jealousy at the thought of the two of them together.

Gregory had not looked at a woman in so long, the thought both excited and frightened him. How could he even be thinking about her in this way? Yet, how could he stop?

A cup of tea sounded good to relax him enough so he could sleep. The light was on upstairs. He gritted his teeth and opened the door to shut it off. It bothered him that Joel went to sleep with the light on and radio playing. He usually left the radio on, not wanting to climb the stairs.

He went back to the kitchen. Stirring sugar into his tea, he took a big swallow without thinking, burning his mouth. He nearly dropped the cup.

He prayed, *God, what's wrong with me? I never burn my mouth, and rarely do I have insomnia.*

Yet he sort of liked the dizzy feeling, the way his mind kept going to Laura, the way he looked for ways to see more of her.

As it was now, he saw her during church services, but that didn't count. They were never alone; someone was always breaking in with various comments. If she came over for dinner or they went to Ruth's, the boys were front and center.

He reminisced back to when he'd first felt love for a woman. Always in his mind were thoughts of Beth Marie. Beth Marie with the beautiful green eyes, following her mother's advice and marrying a man with "more promise."

Lord, if You want me to follow You, please put it into Beth Marie's heart, too, he had prayed as a young, brash man, sure, yet unsure of himself.

Either God had not put it in her heart or Beth Marie had not listened, because her wedding took place at the end of summer. Though he was invited, Gregory stayed away from both the ceremony and reception. Knowing she had chosen another was devastating enough without seeing her in person, all smiles, looking at and kissing another man. *How could she?* had drummed through his head over the years. They had been everything to each other. How could he put her softness out of his mind? How could he ever hope to love another?

He was accepted at a seminary in California. He wanted to get out of North Dakota. He'd been teased about his Midwest twang, and it took weeks of practicing before he sounded like the others. When he reached Joseph, he was ready and eager to serve his first congregation.

Though he wasn't ready to forget Beth Marie, Shirley was there, so helpful, so positive and patient. And God had blessed them with two sons.

He thought again about Joel, how he still irritated him; but suddenly some of the things that bothered him didn't seem important. Why did he always make a big fuss about Joel's leaving the light and the radio on? There were worse things the kid could be doing. And he made good grades. He'd be in line for a scholarship if he kept on progressing well.

He remembered that afternoon at church. He had listened to Caleb's piano playing. The boy pounded, but that was okay. He had a good touch, he'd overheard Laura say. He was glad Caleb had chosen to take lessons.

But it was Joel's coming each week that had shocked him. He had no idea he would agree to playing a solo. Laura hadn't known Gregory was just outside the door, listening as she spoke to Joel. And Joel, always the quiet, unresponsive son, had talked. Unbelievable. He'd wanted to go out and praise his eldest son, but something kept him there, hidden. Many times he longed to pull Joel close, just hold him for a long moment, but he always stopped. Was it the boy's expression, his don't-touch-me attitude? His pulling away the few times Gregory had reached out? Soon he had stopped trying. Maybe he shouldn't have. But how did one turn back the clock and start over again? You had one chance with a marriage, one chance with a kid. If you failed, you couldn't undo the wrong.

Or could you? God never gave up on His children. How could Gregory?

The cup was empty and he still wasn't sleepy. He opened his Bible to the psalms. Some pages slipped out. "Time to buy a new Bible, I think." He could order one from the local bookstore, but he needed to go to La Grande to buy a piano. Maybe Laura would accompany him for the day.

Humming, he set his cup in the sink and padded back to bed. For some reason he suddenly felt better. Yes, Mrs. Laura Madison had made a difference to the Hall family, the church, and most of all to Gregory's heart.

twelve

Laura walked over to the church to practice Friday morning. A guest soloist was scheduled and had brought the sheet music. Laura wasn't familiar with the song and felt she needed to go over it a few times. Then, too, she wanted to plan a lesson book for Caleb to practice when he came to use the piano at the church. She hoped Gregory found a used piano soon. Caleb needed to be able to practice at home.

"Laura!" Gregory stood in the doorway motioning her. "Phone. Kenny Thompson."

Laura cringed. They hadn't dated yet because Kenny had been gone on a business trip.

"Probably wants to ask you out again," Gregory said as Laura moved past him.

"Why would he call me here?"

"I'm sure Ruth told him where you were."

She wished Gregory would leave the office, but he was intent on shuffling through papers, pretending not to pay attention. If only the church owned a portable phone.

"Mr. Thompson?" Laura knew her cheeks were flushed. She took a deep breath. "The movie in Enterprise? Oh, yes, I understood fully about the sick little calf and the business trip."

She turned her back so she wouldn't see Gregory's expression. He'd make her laugh. Laura wished Kenny had never asked her out, nor should she have consented to have lunch with him. She didn't want to hurt him but should have explained she was happy in her single state. He seemed like the type who could be overbearing. She looked over to see Gregory penciling a big "YES."

Laura left church shortly after. Her mood for playing the piano had disappeared.

"What does one wear on a date?" she asked Ruth later. The last time she'd dated was back in the early seventies.

"I'd go conservative," Ruth said. "How about your dark slacks and that nice pastel pink blouse?"

"What do you suppose he'll wear?"

"Jeans, denim jacket, cowboy boots, and of course his hat. The same thing he wears to church. Most ranchers and farmers around here have one attire. Jeans with dirt and cow dung for day wear, clean jeans for church and dates."

"Ruth! Cow dung. How awful."

"You can't miss it, hon."

She remembered how Kenny stuck out in church, being the only one who wore a cowboy hat.

"Wear just a touch of makeup," Ruth added.

Laura changed to a pink, ruffled blouse and sweater vest, then back to a forest green light top and tan slacks.

One thing about Kenny Thompson, he was punctual. Since Laura had changed clothes three times, she was not ready. She heard Kenny and Ruth chatting in the living room as she hurried down the stairs. She never had liked making a grand entrance, nor did she like being late.

Kenny stood, hat in hand, his other hand reaching out to shake hers. "I see you're ready." His smile was hearty, his dark eyes almost smoldering. She'd forgotten he was so short and stocky.

"Yes."

"We don't want to be late. One thing I can't stand is walking into a movie house once the lights are dimmed."

"I totally agree," Laura said. It was the last complete sentence she uttered.

"I expect you want to hear about the ranch and what I do

there and that sort of thing," he said as held the car door open. It wasn't his truck; a Cadillac, yellow with wire wheels, waited in front of the bed-and-breakfast. It shone as if he'd polished on it half a day.

"This is my first nice car, and it's been a dandy." He removed his hat for a second, then stuck it back on. "Course I never drive it. I prefer the truck or the Jeep."

"It's nice—"

"Well, back to the ranch; I was born in the very house I now live in. I'm an only son, have one sister who lives in Alaska. Haven't seen her since Ma was buried about three years ago now. I do all my cooking, housecleaning, washing clothes, riding the herd, checking fences. I'm my own boss from one end to the other."

"I see you like ranch life—"

"Shucks, I wouldn't have it any other way. I sometimes think of having a little filly there, cooking my breakfast and taking care of my needs, but most of 'em don't know how to cook nowadays." He glanced at Laura, who was trying to disappear into the seat cushion. "You know how to cook, Laura?"

"Well, I—"

Before she could answer, he was off and running. "That's okay. You play a mean piano and that counts for a lot."

Laura was relieved to see the outskirts of Enterprise. She did not like the way this was going, and they'd only driven seven miles. Kenny Thompson pretty well put his wants and needs on the line. It was her wildest nightmare. He assumed she knew he was looking for someone. Why else would he have asked her out? One didn't spend money on a "filly" if it wasn't for a reason.

He pulled into the parking lot and hopped out to hold her door open. "I've always believed in opening the door for a woman. My pa taught me that when I was this high." He held his hand out. "C'mon, let's mosey on over there." He took her hand and she followed because she had to.

It was a big, callused hand, a strong hand. She couldn't have extricated her hand from his grip if she'd wanted to.

"Hiya, there, Trudy. This here's Laura, the new piano teacher over in Joseph. Been there a while, going to stay a bit longer—"

Laura forced a smile as she looked at the older woman taking tickets. "Just five minutes until the show starts. Better get your popcorn now," she said, nodding at Laura.

Kenny ordered a barrel of popcorn with two squirts of butter, two Cokes, and a large candy bar. Laura took her drink and the candy and followed him inside.

She couldn't remember later what the movie was about. She kept moving to the far side of the seat as Kenny kept leaning toward her. She let him eat the popcorn, and he ate the whole tub. She found herself thinking about the first time she and Jerry had gone to the movies, how shy they both had been. How she couldn't even quite look at him or he at her.

As the movie went on, Laura remembered "Bridge Over Troubled Waters" as being their favorite song. They'd met on a Tuesday and Jerry was constantly humming the Moody Blues' tune, "Tuesday, Tuesday." But Kenny liked country and western music. On the way here, she'd listened to Billy Ray Cyrus singing about his "Achy Breaky Heart." And Garth Brooks bellowed out something about "The River." Kenny told her they were old songs he'd put on a cassette.

"You enjoyin' this movie?" Kenny asked, loud enough for everyone to hear. " 'Cause if not, we can always pick up a video and go back to my place."

She cringed farther into the seat. How could this be happening? She, a woman of forty-five, out on a date, feeling worse than when she was a teenager. How was she going to get out of going back to his house?

"Actually, I'm enjoying the scenery in the movie," she said, hoping that would sound truthful. And the Montana landscape was beautiful. Of course there were horses in the movie. Laura doubted that Kenny would enjoy a movie without horses or cows.

Afterwards, Kenny took her to his favorite place for ice cream, waving to everyone he saw. He knew all the local people, since he'd lived in the area all his life.

"You're quiet," he said; but before Laura could answer, he began telling about the woman he'd almost married, the one who'd died in a car accident over on the road going to Troy. "Never did find out why she was going to Troy. There's nothing there but a motel and a place for hunters to camp, and fishing in the summer."

"I'm sorry about your loss."

"Well, it's been a long time now. A lot of water has gone under the bridge. And over it!" He laughed then. "Yeah, lots of women around, but I never paid much attention to any of them. But there was something about you, the way you play the piano and all."

Laura licked the butterscotch sauce off her spoon. She wanted more than anything for this night to be over.

"You're a widow, Pastor tells me."

"Yes. We were married twenty years."

"When did he die?"

"Five years ago."

"Then you're probably ready to git married again."

Laura swallowed, then choked on the sweet, gooey sauce. She tried to catch her breath, but coughed harder than ever. "I—I—"

"Don't try to talk." He jumped up and pounded her so hard on the back she thought he'd broken her spine.

Her face was red, her eyes watered, and worse than anything was the awareness that everyone in the place was watching her. She wanted to climb into a hole and hide. At last she had her voice again. "I shouldn't try to eat and talk at the same time."

"I didn't mean to get you all excited. About getting married again, I mean." His hand stole across the table and took hers.

"Mr. Thompson—"

"Kenny. Call me Kenny. Everyone does."

"Kenny, you're a very nice person, but I have no plans to remarry. That's a big step, and I'm quite happy with my life the way it is."

He leaned back and shifted his hat, a habit she found particularly annoying. "People change their minds."

The ride home was a silent one. She expected him to talk more about the ranch, and when she asked what he grew, he hit the steering wheel. "Mint," was all he said. When Joseph came into view, Laura felt relief. At least she wouldn't have to worry about his asking her out again.

He pulled up in front of the dark house, turned the lights off, and put his arm around the back of the seat. He didn't touch her, but she could feel the warmth of his arm, no more than an inch from her shoulder.

"I'm a decent sort of guy. You could do worse than me."

"Mr.—I mean, Kenny, do you believe in God?"

He reared forward as if he couldn't believe she'd asked that.

"Believe in God? Who don't believe in God?"

"Lots of people."

"Of course I believe in God. You saw me in church, didn't you?"

She nodded. "Many people attend church, but it doesn't mean they believe in salvation or have accepted Jesus into their heart."

"Well, I don't know about the salvation or accepting Jesus, but I do believe in God and I believe that Reverend Gregory is a good man."

"Goodness doesn't get you to heaven."

He opened the door and was around to her side before she realized it.

"I'll think about what you said. And I'll be calling you." He took off his hat, leaned over, and kissed her on the cheek. "Thanks for going to the movie with me. I'll see you again."

Oh, please, Laura wanted to cry out, but she said nothing as he walked back to the car and hopped in. She let herself in and sank into the nearest sofa close to the door. If only Ruth were up so they could talk. More than anything, she needed to discuss this over a cup of tea.

Ruth moved out of the shadows of the sitting room. "I heard the car door slam."

"Oh, Ruth."

"What?" Ruth looked expectant.

"He wants a woman. I don't know if he wants marriage, but he definitely wants a woman, and I know I'm not that woman."

For the second time that night, Laura found herself thinking of Jerry and the love they'd had, the marriage that had been wonderful and sacred. She thought of Gregory and how his quiet nature both delighted and frustrated her. She wanted him to bare his soul. Well, after tonight, perhaps she didn't. Kenny Thompson had bared his soul and there hadn't been time for anything else. He was a rich and, in her opinion, an egotistical, overbearing man.

"At least you saw a movie."

Laura giggled. "I can't even tell you one thing it was about."

"No?" Ruth poured water into cups. "I guess it was a dud, then?"

"A real bomb, Ruth. A real bomb."

"Sometimes first dates are like that. I can remember a few."

"No. It's just that I feel we are from two different planets. I know nothing about ranching, and he knows nothing about my life or what I deem important."

"Maybe you have to tell him."

Laura sighed. "Ruth, the man talks nonstop. Did you realize that?"

"No, honey, I didn't. But, then, it's probably because I've never said more than a few words to Mr. Kenny Thompson."

"He would make some woman a terrific husband, I'm sure of it, but she'd need earplugs."

Ruth looked at her and they both burst into laughter.

"Now I'm getting silly."

"Let's go to bed then. Tomorrow is another day and you know what that means."

"No, what?"

"A day to praise God, to be thankful for our blessings, and a day to go to Enterprise for supplies!"

The women laughed again, linking their arms as they went down the hall.

thirteen

The days went fast for Laura. She couldn't believe so much had taken place in such a short time. She'd come wanting to find a new life for herself, to be of service and a blessing to people.

One day a week she read to Mrs. Yates, an elderly member of the church who was nearly blind and needed someone to write letters to her sister in Seattle. She looked in on others who wanted to remain independent and could do so if someone checked on them on a regular basis. Laura also tutored a physically challenged child whose mother preferred to keep her at home. She drove Ruth to Enterprise once a week for supplies for the bed-and-breakfast. She now had four piano students and could have had more, but since she hadn't come to Joseph to simply be "kept busy," she declined. Laura loved to be needed and knew it was God's plan all along.

The time between 1:30 and 3:30 was free. She often strolled through town, stopping by to say hello to Nancy at the bookstore or stopping for a latte. For some reason, she strolled toward the church that afternoon.

There was a light on under Gregory's office door, so she wondered if her practicing would bother him. He usually left the office when Caleb had his lesson, not that she said he must, but he decided it was better for Caleb.

She tapped on the door.

He boomed, "Come in," and she entered to find him poring over a book sitting on a stack of five or six volumes.

"I didn't mean to disturb you, but—"

"No, not at all. You're saving me from a boring time of

looking up some information."

She pulled out the chair he indicated and glanced up, her eyes meeting his steady gaze.

"It's just that I wanted to practice a bit—sort of at loose ends, I guess."

"Your playing will definitely not disturb me." He drummed on the open book with the eraser end of a new pencil.

Laura started to get up, but he pleaded with her to stay. "I want to throw a couple of things at you, if you don't mind."

"Sure, what gives?"

The office was immaculate. A bookcase filled with an assortment of books covered the wall under the window. A flowered, ruffled curtain covered the top half. He'd told her earlier that Ruth had made the curtains and had overseen the decorating of his office when he first arrived in Joseph. It was not only clean, but a comfortable place.

"Hope you don't mind sitting for a minute," he said, pointing toward the door. "Glad you left the door open. People do tend to talk in small towns."

Laura smiled. Imagine anyone linking her with the pastor. Not only was he too young, it was apparent he was quite happy with his celibate relationship.

"How can I be of help?"

He drummed the pencil on the book again. "I'd like you to listen to the opening paragraph of this coming Sunday's sermon."

"Very well. Go ahead."

Laura leaned back, crossing her legs while she waited for him to begin. This was a first. He'd never asked her advice on anything with the exception of what to do about Joel's sullenness.

"I very much admire the writings of Dietrich Bonhoeffer. I quote him often."

"Wasn't he involved in World War II?"

"Yes, very much so. He was German and stood up against Hitler and what he was doing to Germany. His beliefs got him executed. My sermon topic concerns our doing what is important, standing up for your beliefs and making your actions count. But my sermon has no life. I must make it come to life, to show the marvelous teachings of this man."

"Use some quotes," Laura suggested. "You sound pretty impassioned to me."

Gregory looked surprised. "I'm a World War II buff."

Laura nodded, her interest piqued. "Read me what you have so far."

He read the quote and summed it up in his own words. He was right. It didn't come to life, and she wasn't sure why.

"I was wondering if you'd ever thought of coming down from the pulpit and standing on the main floor?"

Gregory almost looked shocked. "You mean walk down as I'm talking or start from that vantage point?"

Laura cleared her throat. "Either way works." She could see that Gregory wasn't keen on the idea. Not that he put himself above the people of his church, but he tended to go strictly by protocol, meaning one stood in the pulpit. Always.

"It's just an idea."

"Is that where the pastor stood in your church back in Sealand?"

"Sometimes."

He seemed to be thinking this over. "I guess it would take some getting used to. Maybe he felt uncomfortable the first time he did it."

"Yes, maybe so."

"I shouldn't be a pastor—"

"Don't be ridiculous," Laura broke in. "You are great with your people and they know they can count on you to come for any crisis and pray with them when needed. I feel that one of the most important parts of a ministry is being there when needed. A lot of pastors fail that part of the calling."

He nodded and leaned back in the chair. She'd noticed this before and each time held her breath, hoping the chair wouldn't go clear back, sending Gregory crashing to the floor.

"I try to do what is required of a minister."

"So, back to the sermon."

"Could you read it?"

"I'd be happy to."

"It won't be taking you from any other duty?"

She laughed. "Not hardly. You know my time is pretty much my own since coming here. That's how I wanted it, yet I like helping others."

"And you certainly do that." Gregory leaned forward. "What do you think of Joseph by now?"

Laura laughed again. "I love the people, and the scenery is awe-inspiring." She looked at the pages in her hand. She'd once suggested he might type up his sermon, as once in a while there'd be a long pause in the sermon while he was trying to decipher his notes. That was another reason, she knew, for his not wanting to walk down among the people. Where would he put his notes? She wondered again how he would do if he didn't depend on the notes. What if he spoke from the heart? Would that mean as much to the people? Wouldn't they get just as much out of his talk?

"I'll read this in the fellowship hall and get it back to you before Caleb comes for his lesson."

"I'm not putting you out now—"

She paused in the doorway, looking back. Something about the look on his face gave her the sudden urge to go over and smooth the hair back, to reassure him that things would work out, that they always would with God in control. She resisted the urge.

Noticing her hesitancy, he stood and walked over. "I need

to say one thing, Laura, if I may." He was close enough for her to touch that lock of hair, but she didn't. Their eyes met and held.

"Yes?"

"You've done a lot of good for my boys and this church, and I wanted you to know I appreciate it." Before she could respond, he bent down and swiftly brushed his lips against her forehead.

His action so surprised her that she stood immobilized, unable to speak. Gregory was the first to step back. "I know you have things to do. I–I—" He didn't finish his sentence.

Laura's fingers gripped the pages of the sermon notes as she turned and hurriedly left the room.

She decided to make a cup of instant coffee. As the water sang in the teakettle on the stove, she wondered about the kiss. Gregory was appreciative, that was all. He didn't care for her. She knew he thought she was far too outspoken.

Stirring the coffee over and over, her gaze fell on the page with hastily scribbled notes. If only she could convince him he needed to update things. Why not do research on the Internet instead of checking out all those books? She was sure he could find scads of information on this Bonhoeffer.

Laura read two paragraphs, then knew she would make this a special project. She'd use the computer at the bookstore and E-mail her request to a friend in Portland, asking for the needed information. She'd surprise Gregory with it in the next day or so. Perhaps not in time to incorporate into this Sunday's message, but in time for the following week's. If Bonhoeffer was so important, didn't he rate two Sundays?

She read the notes, liking what she read. If anything, Gregory was thorough in his research. She circled important data, then took it upon herself to begin anew. She boxed off the Scripture to the left, like a sidebar, and numbered the points he made, then summarized the contents into one large paragraph at the bottom. She wrote the major points and wrote, *Add to this info from your own words.*

Numbering the pages, she stacked them together with a paper clip. A note scrawled on a separate sheet of paper should encourage him.

> *Great research, Gregory. I think this topic needs two Sundays. Why not continue on with it for one more week? What a great man he was! Hope you like my number system. L*

He was gone when she walked back to the office. A note on the door said he'd be there at 8:00 A.M. the following morning. In case of emergency, please call the nursing home in Enterprise. She slipped the notes on top of his desk, covered them with a notepad, and left the room. But not before she paused long enough to gaze at two boys smiling from five-by-seven photos. How he loved those boys, yet he had a problem showing it. Not once had she seen him hug Joel. Caleb received hugs and attention only because he was younger and demanded attention from his father. *The squeaky wheel gets the grease,* Laura thought. She looked at Shirley again. The smile was genuine, but there was a look in the eyes Laura wondered about. What had she really been like? Had she been happy as Gregory's wife?

She noticed a new framed quotation and paused to read it:

> *Life is mostly froth and bubble,*
> *Two things stand like stone:*
> *Kindness in another's trouble,*
> *Courage in our own.*
>
> > *—Adam Lindsay Gordon*

"I like that," Laura said aloud. "That's a good thought. I

wonder who this Adam Lindsay Gordon is."

She closed the door and went to the piano. Playing eased her feelings, soothed her emotions. She remembered those teen years before they'd moved to Oregon, how she'd played; she remembered a happy time when she had played for that small church in the farming town in Nebraska. How she'd loved playing the dear old hymns. They were hymns that a lot of churches didn't play today. Not that she minded those from time to time, but sometimes she missed the songs of Charles Wesley and Fanny Crosby. She felt many old hymns offered more substance than some of the newer songs.

Her mother had loved "When the Roll Is Called Up Yonder," but "Onward, Christian Soldiers" had been the most requested at the small church in Nebraska. It always made Laura want to march around the church, just as "The Battle Hymn of the Republic" did. At that thought, she pounded into the song.

She didn't hear the door open nor did she realize that someone was there, listening, until she heard the floor creak at the end of the latest hymn.

"My goodness, but I never tire of hearing you play." Ruth stood as if transfixed. "I brought a spot of my sun tea over and some freshly baked cookies. Thought you and Caleb might like a snack before you tackle his lesson." She sat on a nearby pew, shaking her head. "Your heart is in your playing. I've never heard anything so beautiful. And if the board of trustees ever says we need an organ, I'm going to veto it with both hands."

"Ruth, you're a peach." Laura left the bench and closely encircled the plump woman's body. "I don't know how I'd get along without you. And I agree with you about the piano."

The side door burst open and Caleb rushed in. Cheeks flushed, he shoved a paper under Laura's nose. "See? I did what you said. I studied before that test and I got a perfect 100!"

"Caleb, I'm so proud of you!"

He beamed while Ruth hugged him, too. "I knew there was a reason to bake something special this afternoon."

"Where's Dad?"

"Gone to the nursing home, probably to visit Bernice," Ruth said.

"Oh, yeah, that's right. But sometimes he waits until I get here."

"You can show him the minute your lesson is over." Laura faced the young boy. "Did you practice your scales like I suggested?"

"Yes, I did."

"And you're ready to start in?"

"Just as soon as I wash my hands."

"Boy, he's wired. Hope you can get him to settle down for a lesson."

"He'll do just fine."

"I'll see you tonight. For supper?"

Laura nodded. "For supper, yes."

Caleb returned, sat on the bench, posed his hands just right, and began the scales. Laura hummed as he ran up and down the keys. Scales loosened up the fingers and the mind. She noted he held his fingers arched, bent just a bit at the knuckle. His back was straight, his head held high. So far he'd taken to all her instruction. Caleb was a child easy to like. She just wished that Joel was as likable. But maybe someday. Maybe someday both he and his father would realize how wonderful they actually were.

Laura smiled as her fingers felt the place on her forehead. Gregory had kissed her there. The gesture touched her deeply and she wasn't quite sure why. . . .

fourteen

"Do you still want to play the solo, Joel?" Laura asked after several rehearsals. She tried to smile as she stared at his somber face. It was as if she were looking at a blank wall. "The most difficult part is knowing when to start, then later come in. All you need to do is watch me and I'll nod or point if that helps."

"Yeah, I guess so," he finally said, his eyes not quite meeting Laura's.

Laura leaned forward. "Are you doing this for your father? Because you think he wants you to?"

He said nothing.

"I could probably tell him I'll just play the piece the regular way without trumpet accompaniment." She stifled a sigh of discouragement, remembering how hard it was reaching a child when he didn't want to do something but wouldn't admit it. Like going out for a sport or the class play: If she thought it was a good idea, her children would go ahead and do it, then grump all through the season or practice.

"I know you can do a fine job, if that's what worries you. I say go for it. We'll practice as many times as you wish."

There. She'd made a decision for him.

He shrugged. "One more time, then I'm outta here."

"Fine."

Joel stood straight and tall, shoulders thrust back. His face was thin, his whole body lean and hard. The blond hair hung into his eyes, but the back was sheared off as so many of the boys were wearing their hair now. It probably wasn't the most becoming, but if it made him feel good, why not?

There was one tiny bit of hesitation at the second part, but he came through loud, strong, and clear.

"That's going to send chills up people's spines on Sunday," Laura said, wanting more than anything to reassure the boy. "And we still have lots of time to practice."

"Yeah." He carefully wiped the mouthpiece and rubbed the golden body of his instrument. Not once, but twice, using circular motions as he polished it. He was treating his trumpet as if it was his love, his lifeline.

Laura remembered a boy and his sax, a daughter who played clarinet. All her kids had played in the school band. Only Kurt still occasionally took out his sax and played. She knew he could have found a band to play with, but every time she suggested it, he'd shrugged. "Or church. Why not play a solo some Sunday?" He'd really groaned at that one.

Oh, yes, she knew about kids who needed more than anything to talk but kept the words and thoughts bottled up inside. Kurt had never shared his feelings with his father, but Gregory was all Joel had. She doubted that he talked to him. She sensed he was like a gun cocked and ready to go off.

Joel laid his trumpet in the case and snapped it closed.

"We'll practice on Thursday directly after school," she called after his retreating back.

"Yeah. Okay."

He closed the door and the inside of the church was silent again. Laura loved the shape of the sanctuary. It was a wonderful setup and would seat at least one hundred, though the church membership was less than that.

Laura opened the hymnal and played the selection Gregory felt would go along with his sermon that Sunday.

Be Thou my vision
O, Lord of my heart. . .

It was the third verse that had always spoken to Laura's heart.

Riches I heed not, nor man's empty praise;
Thou mine inheritance, now and always;
Thou and Thou only first in my heart,
High King of heaven, my treasure Thou art.

Laura's fingers rippled over the keys as she changed tempo and played a spiritual. *Come stand by me, Lord, yes, come stand by me. . .* Laura played a medley, adding some of the later tunes her kids had loved.

She didn't know how long she played nor did she realize she had an audience until clapping sounded from the back of the sanctuary. She whirled around to find Harvey, the custodian, standing there smiling.

"My mother used to play like that," he said, walking down toward her. "We had a piano at home and she'd practice each night. I'd fall asleep to the sound of her playing. I wish you could have met her."

"My mother played, too," Laura said, the emptiness filling her as it often did when she thought of her mother. "I wish she were alive today to come to this beautiful church and to play one Sunday."

"At least we have our memories."

Laura smiled. "Yes, that we do."

"I came to measure the pastor's office. The board met and voted to put in new carpeting for his birthday."

"His birthday? When is that?"

"Last day of June."

Laura rose from the bench, scooting it back. "Sounds like a great gift to me. I trust it's a surprise?"

Harvey nodded. "Yes, that's why I came now while he's at the school giving a talk to the graduating class."

"Oh. I forgot about that."

"I'll see you Sunday," Harvey said with a tip of his cap.

Laura thought about Gregory's birthday, wondering what she might give him as a surprise. What did one give one's pastor? Some were easy to buy for, but not him. She no more knew what he'd like than a perfect stranger. In many ways, he was a stranger.

Then she thought of the bakery in Elgin. It was a fair piece there, but she was ready to head off somewhere. If the boys had a photo, she could mail it to the lady, have her bake the cake, and then pick it up the day before his birthday. That would be a unique gift, one nobody else would give. Laura hummed as she walked down the steps and across the road to home. She'd run the idea by Ruth, knowing Ruth wouldn't breathe a word to anyone.

"I think the cake is a perfect idea," Ruth said, "though I could bake one twice as good I bet. But I sure can't put no photo on it."

Laura paused, her coffee cup in midair. She always had a cup the minute she entered the house. "I think we should have a potluck after church, and you know we need more than one cake, anyway. This will be the centerpiece, and you and perhaps someone else could bake a cake. You can never have too much birthday cake."

Ruth clasped her hands like a little kid who'd just found a bike under the Christmas tree. "I love to plan parties. I'll get a few women busy on the decorations. We didn't do anything last year for Pastor's birthday, so it's high time."

Ruth started on a list while Laura changed into more comfortable clothes. She still worried about Joel, wondering if he really would do okay with the solo on Father's Day.

On Thursday, Joel arrived five minutes early. He nodded in Laura's direction, and she thought his scowl seemed less grim.

"Hello," she said with a nod. Laura knew one never probed,

as there was nothing that made a kid withdraw quicker than a probe, no matter how friendly.

"Hello," he grunted back. He removed his trumpet and it looked shinier than before.

"I never wanted to play trumpet," he said then.

"You didn't?"

"No. It was Dad's idea."

"What would you have chosen?"

"Nothin'."

"I see. Well, shall we start in?"

Laura played the opening two bars. She stopped, then nodded at Joel.

His notes were loud and clear and his head seemed even higher than before. She relaxed just a bit. He lowered his horn and she played the first refrain:

God of our Fathers, Whose almighty hand
Leads forth in beauty all the starry band
Of shining worlds in splendor through the skies,
Our grateful songs before Thy throne arise.

The piece went well and Joel's clear, high notes definitely added something to the old hymn. Laura's hair stood up on the back of her neck.

"That was very good," she said as she played the fourth and final stanza. "Shall we practice again on Saturday?"

He nodded and slumped off, not bothering to remove the mouthpiece or dry off his instrument. The door banged, and she wondered what she'd said or done to make him react that way.

Laura was busy the next few days helping Ruth with the house, as two rooms were rented for that weekend.

"Have no idea what's going on in town. Nothing I know about, but I'm happy for the business."

Laura smiled. "The word has spread about your wonderful pineapple-mango muffins."

"Think I'll make banana."

"Don't you dare!" Laura cried.

Saturday morning she left the guests sitting around the circular oak dining room table, partaking of more of Ruth's muffins, egg and ham omelets, and the rich brewed coffee she bought at the new coffee shop in town.

"I must dash. Time to practice the opening hymn."

"Perhaps you'd both like to attend the service tomorrow. It promises to be a great one, the music, that is," Ruth said to both sets of guests.

Laura didn't hear their answer as she closed the door and ran down the steps.

Joel was waiting at the church.

"Am I late?" She glanced at her watch, knowing she was not. It was the one thing she prided herself on: being on time.

"Nope!" He ran a hand through his shock of hair.

"Well, let's get this show on the road."

"You're funny," he said then.

She looked up from the hymnal, her eyes leaving the page numbers. "Funny? In what way?"

He shrugged. "Just the things you say. What you do."

Was this a compliment? Laura wondered. She had no way of knowing. "My kids always said I was a bit spacey."

He set his horn on the pew and glanced up with such a pensive look that Laura yearned to reach out to hug him.

"I can't talk to my father."

"Why not, Joel?"

"He doesn't understand. He never has."

"What is it you need to talk about?"

"Just things."

Did she dare ask more, or would it make him stop talking? "Do you want to talk to me about it?"

He grabbed his horn and shook his head. "No. Forget I said anything. Sometimes I say too much."

Laura knew it must be difficult for him not having a mother who cared, a mother who would praise him. She knew Gregory was a good father but doubted that he thought praising his sons was part of the job. Caleb didn't need praises, but Joel was a different matter.

The rest of the practice went fine, though the smile she'd caught a glimpse of earlier disappeared and the serious scowl took its place. If only he'd talk! But at least she had let him know she was available. Look at the progress they'd made this week: from not speaking, to a half-smile, to his opening up just a bit this morning.

The solo went well and she smiled, giving the A-OK sign with thumb and index finger.

"I have to leave. There's a meeting at school at one."

"See you Sunday morning," Laura called to his retreating back. She wanted to talk more but knew he had said all he was going to for this time. She was amazed he'd even mentioned the meeting. Before, he just went, not offering any explanation.

She went over the hymns again, then left the church. Today she would not have lunch at Ruth's but would go to The Book Corner and have a cup of coffee and one of their huge cookies. For some reason that sounded good.

As she walked, she wondered what Gregory's Father's Day sermon would be about. She also wondered if he would appreciate the special music, the time and effort his son had made learning the piece, then standing up in front of the congregation when it scared him more than a little. She would make certain that Gregory commented to his son his appreciation. She wondered, also, if the boys had thought of buying their father a gift for Father's Day. So often it was the mother's role to make sure gifts were bought and presented, thank you notes written.

She opened the door and slipped inside the coffee shop, her favorite stop in all of Joseph.

"Good afternoon, Laura!" came the cheerful voice. "The usual?"

"Yes, but make it a double latte today. I think I need it."

fifteen

A house for rent was becoming available the first of July, and Laura discussed the possibility of moving with Ruth one afternoon while they were both in the kitchen baking for that night's youth party. The Joseph youth were meeting with the youth in Enterprise.

The Father's Day service had gone well, with many accolades for Joel. He'd stood proud and tall, and Laura thought she detected a tear in Gregory's eye. She overheard him telling Joel later what a good job he'd done and then beamed when Joel gave her the credit.

The following Sunday they'd celebrated Gregory's birthday with a potluck, and the cake from the bakery in Elgin had been a big hit. The photo was one of him and his sons with the Wallowa Mountains as a backdrop.

While Laura and Ruth were talking, the doorbell rang. Before Laura could answer, Caleb popped in. "I heard there were cookies to sample."

Ruth motioned for him to come to the table and poured him a glass of milk.

"I'll be glad when I'm old enough to go to the youth meetings." He bit into a chocolate chip cookie, then frowned. "Not bad, Laura. Almost as good as Ruth's."

She reached to swat him, but he ducked out of the way.

"I'm going," he said. "I'll be back tonight 'cause I'm not staying alone."

"Good. Maybe we can play a game," Laura said.

Ruth was also setting bread to rise. Someone had offered her a bread machine, which she refused. "I like making my own bread. Just doesn't seem right if I don't knead it."

"So, you're moving out, deserting me in my hour of need," said Ruth, returning to the topic of the house.

"You could rent out my room in an instant, and you know it." Laura stacked the cool cookies. "Besides, it's time I learned to fly solo again."

&

Laura had finally received a letter from Jen and a phone call from Kurt. It was ironic that he asked again when she was coming home. He didn't realize how much this was becoming home to her. She had recently added two more students to her schedule, bringing it to a total of six now. Each was progressing nicely and she enjoyed the lessons.

Since the cookies and cake were done and nothing was pressing, Laura walked toward town. She and Joel walked one afternoon a week. It had happened quite by accident.

She'd been on her way to the bookstore one day after school when he caught up with her.

"I never thanked you—"

"Thanked me? What do you mean?"

"For helping me with the solo."

"Oh, that." She turned and their eyes met. Joel seldom looked her in the eye. She felt she'd crossed an important step. She thought of the first practice with Joel. It had been hard working with a morose boy who grunted barely audible replies to her questions. He at least looked at her during the second practice, and by the third practice, had actually smiled.

"You did a wonderful job as you already know," she said now.

"Lots of people said so," he affirmed.

"I knew it would go well. I had every confidence in you. And not even one mistake!"

"Almost did."

"But you didn't and that's the important thing."

"I couldn't have done it without your help."

"I enjoyed it, as you must know. Are you happy with the trumpet, Joel? Remember you said it was all your father's idea—"

"I was just saying that. I like it fine."

"That's great because I think you have a natural bent."

He beamed but said nothing.

ঌ

The late June sun beat out of a cloudless sky, causing Laura to shade her face with her hand as she greeted Joel. She could never bring herself to wear a shady hat, though she'd been told to more than once.

"Say, let's drive out to the lake and say hi to the Boeves. Want to?"

"Sure."

"A chocolate peanut butter ice cream sounds good to me right now. You can get your piece of fudge and I'll bring a slice back to enjoy later. Should we leave a note for your father?"

"Nah. He knows I'm around."

The deer were waiting out front for people food.

"Hello, friends," Laura called. "We couldn't stand another minute without ice cream and fudge."

Oliver looked up and smiled. "Made a fresh batch last night. It's going fast this week. Here, try my new recipe. It has apples in it."

"Yum!" both Laura and Joel agreed.

"Hello, Joel, Laura," Keithanne said with a wave, after helping a customer. "How are things going with you two?"

"Summer blahs, I think," Laura responded. "My son called last night wanting to know when I was coming home."

Keithanne handed over a double-decker chocolate peanut butter. "Once a mother, always a mother, right?"

Joel had gone to a far aisle to look at some merchandise.

"I cannot believe Joel came with you and he actually looks happy," Keithanne added in a lower voice.

Laura moved closer. "We've been walking the past couple of weeks. Talking about things. You know, he's such a neat kid—if he could just open up to his father."

More customers came in, so Laura gave Keithanne a quick hug. "See you next trip."

Laura drove over by the lake. The little park was filled with people.

"Let's just stay here by the car," Joel suggested.

"Sure. Sounds fine to me." Laura leaned against the hood, looking out over the vast lake. She never tired of this spot and the beauty of God's creation. She still hadn't made it to Hell's Canyon, one of the world's great wonders, but it was on her agenda. That and going to Troy. It was quite a trip there, but worth it, according to Kenny. She hadn't dated him again, but they'd become friends and that was fine.

"Did I mention I'm renting the Cooper place?"

Joel stopped digging at the ground with his shoe while a smile crossed his face. "No, but that's good."

"Why do you say that?"

"It means you're staying in Joseph longer."

Laura laughed and reached over and impulsively hugged Joel. He flinched, but only for a moment. She moved away. "I think Ruth's hugging has rubbed off on me."

"It's okay." He didn't look her in the eye. "Maybe we should go back."

Joel was quiet on the way home. Laura respected his need for silence and said nothing. "It's a show of true friendship," Renee had said once, "when people can be together and not feel the need for talk."

Laura dropped Joel off, then went home to help Ruth clean.

"You don't need to do this, Laura."

"I know I don't need to, but I want to. Honest."

"Oh! I almost forgot! Your son called again."

Laura shook her head. "That kid never gives up, does he?"

"It's difficult for some kids when a parent isn't at their beck and call."

"I'm not going back just because he thinks he needs me or has a problem with his job or Susan."

Ruth nodded. "Stick to your guns, is the only advice I can give."

Laura would move the following week. It was going to be a busy week with Independence Day and the annual fireworks show at the lake. She could hardly wait to invite Ruth and the Hall family over for a meal. This was definitely a permanent step, and suddenly she realized how it must look. She also remembered the advice from one of the old-timers: "Better wait until you've gone through a winter here before deciding to stay."

Gregory dropped Caleb off at seven. Dressed in casual pants and a plaid shirt, Gregory looked almost like a kid. Laura trembled when their eyes met.

"I need to go to La Grande Monday. Want to come along?"

"Yes, that sounds wonderful."

"I'm going over to look at a piano; I thought you'd know if it was a good buy."

Of course, Laura thought. He didn't want her company. He needed someone to tell him if it was a good piano, a decent buy. Then she remembered she had a busy day scheduled.

"Maybe you forgot that Caleb's lesson's on Monday."

Gregory ran his hand through his hair. "I already explained you'd have to change the day. With school out, it isn't going to matter."

"I also have another student. Crissie Johnson. Do you know the Johnson family?"

He nodded. "Yes. I've been visiting the Johnsons to invite them to church. She's willing, but Dan has a problem with organized religion."

"I think a lot of people feel that way, Gregory. Don't take it personally."

"Can you put the lesson off to another day?"

"I suppose I could. But I still need to be back by 3:30."

"Why 3:30?"

"That's when I'm helping the Girl Scouts with play practice."

He shook his head. "I think you've gotten to know more people in the nearly three months you've been here than I know after being here fifteen years."

"It's getting that way. I'll call the Johnsons. So when should I be ready?"

"Better make it seven if we have to be back early."

"Need anything in La Grande?" Laura asked Ruth. "We're going over to look at pianos."

Ruth looked up. "Sure. I'll give you a list—a short one. Hey, that's terrific about a piano. Won't Caleb be pleased? Does he know about it yet?"

"No," Gregory said. "I don't want him disappointed in case we don't find one."

Ruth laughed. "I bet you will."

"We will."

Caleb came in, skateboard under arm. "I thought you had to get over there quick."

"I'm going, I'm going."

"Why are you smiling?" Caleb asked, looking at Laura, then Ruth.

"Nothing," both said. "We're just happy folks by nature."

Caleb accepted that along with a glass of milk. "I just figured out," he said, looking up, "if I had two lessons a week, I would be able to play for church in one year instead of two."

Laura looked at him, shaking her head. This kid was thinking every minute. He watched her expectantly, waiting for an answer.

"You're right, Caleb. Practice makes perfect."

"Oh, wow! A year. I can hardly wait. Maybe I'll have a piano by then. If I practiced an hour a day, I could maybe play in six months!"

"All right. That's enough. You make my head spin."

Laura helped clean the kitchen, her heart suddenly light. Monday should be an interesting day.

sixteen

Gregory arrived early and soon they were on their way for the nearly two-hour trip.

"Were your parents farmers?" Laura asked.

They'd just driven out of Enterprise and Laura wanted to know about Gregory's childhood.

"Nope. My father owned a hardware store."

"Mine ran the local grocery store."

"Did you attend summer camp?"

"No, but we had retreats."

"Same here. That's how I met Beth Marie. At a youth retreat."

The seriousness was back, and she noticed how tightly he gripped the steering wheel.

"Beth Marie?"

"We were sort of semi-engaged."

"Oh." Laura stared out the window. Was he going to talk about it? Surely he, as a minister, knew it was better to discuss things than to let them fester away inside.

"She promised to marry me."

"Kids make lots of promises."

"We weren't exactly kids then. I was nineteen."

"Your first love?"

"Yeah. My first serious love."

"And you've not been able to get her out of your mind all these years?"

Gregory took his coffee cup from the holder between their seats and took a sip. "Something like that."

"Then why don't you do something about it?"

"Do something? Such as? What would you suggest?"

Laura tucked her knees up. "All I know is I'd want to find out if I was still carrying a torch for someone."

"She married."

"Maybe something happened. Maybe she's no longer married."

"I don't even know where she lives. Lost all track when my mother died."

"That shouldn't stop you. Look at how people are finding each other, delving into their backgrounds in search of ancestors. You can do lots on the Internet. Put her name out there and see what happens."

He fingered the slight stubble of beard on his chin. "Yes, maybe I should."

Laura pointed. "Look. That man is catching a fish. Let's stop and stretch our legs, okay?" Laura wanted to change the subject. She couldn't imagine feeling that way about somebody all these years. Yet, she knew she had loved Jerry with all her heart; if he had left her at the altar, she would have pined, too.

Everyone was catching steelhead at the fast-flowing river. Laura got a sinking sensation in her stomach. Why had she wanted to stop? Seeing the exuberant smile on the man's face was a painful reminder of how much Jerry had loved fishing. She'd known many times that she should be thankful he died in his boat, doing what he liked best. For every downside there was a good side. That was the good side of his death.

"Seen enough?" Gregory said, walking up next to her. She was aware of his closeness, even more so here than in the car. More so here with the backdrop of high, rocky cliffs, the sound of the rushing stream. Suddenly she had the impulse to turn and touch him. What would it be like to have his arms enfold her? She shook the thought as she turned and raced to the car.

"We're not in that much of a hurry," he said, catching up with her, unlocking her door.

"I know. I just wanted to get the kinks out." She couldn't quite look at him.

"Anytime you want to stop, say the word. I'm not one that gets into a car and drives like a madman until I reach my destination. I've even been known to stop to read historical markers."

"You?" She stared at his profile. "Somehow that surprises me."

"It does, huh?" He looked at her, meeting her gaze.

"It's your turn," Gregory said once they were back on the winding, twisty road.

"My turn?"

"To talk about the love of your life."

"You mean Jerry?"

"Whomever you were married to." He stopped. "Or do you have a secret love in your background?"

She laughed. "Hardly. I knew Jerry was 'the one' on our second date."

"How did you know that?"

"Just the way he was. Thoughtful. Cute. And very much a man of God."

"That was important to you?"

"Definitely. I'd seen marriages fail without God at the helm and knew I must marry a Christian." She nodded at the memory of the tall, gangly boy who had his Bible on the seat beside him when he'd picked her up on their first date. "Besides, it's biblical."

"So it is."

"We knew we wanted to marry, but Jerry wanted to finish college."

"And did he?"

She giggled. "No. We decided not to wait and married at

the end of his sophomore year."

"And he went back and finished while you worked?"

"Are you kidding?" She laughed again at the memory. "I got pregnant right off and it was about that time that his uncle asked if he wanted to go into business with him—"

"Which was?"

"Commercial fishing."

"And he did."

"Yes, and, to make a long story short, he took over the boat when Uncle Al died about ten years ago, and he was happy with that choice. He never wanted to do anything else but fish."

"It must be nice doing what you like and knowing that's what you're supposed to do."

"You don't?" Laura was puzzled. More than once she felt that Gregory questioned his vocation. But if so, why did he continue to preach? God surely would not hold him to a position he didn't feel called to.

"I felt the calling, all right," Gregory said, as if reading Laura's mind. "But somewhere along the way I've had doubts. Major doubts."

"Then it's time to face the issue."

He slowed down and looked at Laura. "Does everything always come so easy to you? Have you always had it all together?"

She bristled at the sound of his voice. "I'm definitely not 'all together' as you put it. Sure I have doubts. Coming here was a big decision and I'm not sure this is where I'm supposed to be."

"Yes, you are."

"What makes you say that?" she sputtered.

"You just fit in. I have an idea you'd fit in wherever you went. Meeting people comes easy for you."

"And not you? Gregory, you're a minister! Ministers have

to like people. It's a prerequisite for the job."

"Why do you suppose I'm still here in Joseph?"

"Because you like it."

"No. Because it's safe. I know the people and they know me. To go somewhere else is terrifying."

She couldn't believe he was saying this. No wonder he had that brooding look most of the time. Down deep he was an insecure person—like his son Joel.

He stopped the car abruptly and pulled off in a turnaround. "I can't talk about this and drive."

"Do you want me to drive?"

"No."

They'd parked up against a rocky incline. Wire fencing jutted along the rock as far as Laura could see. She opened the window, breathing deeply of the fresh mountain air.

"So, do you want to talk about your first love or your future?"

His eyes looked almost wounded. "I've never talked about Beth to anyone, not even Ruth in the early days when I first came to Joseph."

"Why ever not?"

He shrugged. "Why ever should I have? You just don't go around blabbing everything. And especially not when you're a minister and the one who is supposed to listen to others."

"Ruth's a good listener."

"I know, and it's one of your best traits, too."

She was older than Gregory. She found herself wanting to know what other traits he liked, but it was inane to think about it.

"I've let things pretty much happen as they did, knowing God was in control."

"You should be the minister, not me."

"You're a good minister."

"Can't write a decent sermon. You know that's true. Look

how many times you've tightened up my work. Added something of interest. Like that one on Bonhoeffer. You suggested I go two weeks and I received more comments on that than any other sermon, and I even got a letter in the mail."

"The idea is the important thing and you come up with a good one each Sunday."

"Says who?"

"Me."

He eyed her curiously for a long moment. "Well, thank you, I think. I just wanted you to know I appreciate your help."

"I just happen to have a few English skills. Don't ask me how to do square roots, though."

Gregory started the car, and they headed back down the winding highway. There were so many things he wanted to say, but he felt as if a big load had lifted from his shoulders. It felt good to talk about his youth, about Beth Marie. Maybe he would look into finding her on the Internet.

"Let's stop at the bakery in Elgin. You can tell the owner how surprised and pleased you were with the cake."

"Yeah, sounds great."

At the bakery, Gregory watched the process. "Maybe we should order special cakes for the boys' birthdays."

"Just give me ample time," the baker said, removing the cake from under the scanner.

They left with cups of coffee to go.

As they drove on, Gregory realized he wanted the trip to go on forever. He hadn't relaxed or laughed so much in a long time. They even laughed over their lunch at a local small café.

"Is everything all right?" the waitress asked, and this only made Laura laugh more.

"I feel like a school kid," she said, stirring the thick milk shake she'd ordered along with a hamburger and fries.

A curl slipped down on her forehead. He watched to see if she'd brush it out of the way, but she left it there.

"Why are you staring at me like that?" she asked when the waitress came to see if they wanted dessert.

"You're so positive."

"I am?"

"Yes. It's refreshing."

"You could be, too, you know."

"When are you moving?" he asked, as if wanting to change the subject.

"Next week. The place needs some paint and curtains. Maybe a new couch."

"What about your things at the coast? Are you going over to get them?"

"I've considered that, but renting a U-Haul trailer and coming all that way isn't appealing. Think I'd rather pick up something here at the secondhand store."

"Or we could come down to La Grande again; see what they have at the thrift store."

"Just might do that."

The waitress came and Gregory grabbed the bill. Laura just smiled as she slipped two fives out of her purse.

"No way are you paying for this," Gregory insisted.

"Why not? Everyone goes Dutch, you know."

"I don't."

"You should. If anything, people should pay for the pastor's meal."

He finally agreed to let her leave the tip, and they went on their way to look at the advertised piano.

"I like it," Laura said when they looked at it, "even before I play. Such a beautiful ebony." She sat to play, and soon the house was filled with music.

"If you stay here and play every day, I won't sell it," the owner said.

Laura smiled. "This is for a young boy who plays wonderfully well and needs his own piano."

"I'll knock off a hundred dollars and even deliver," the man offered. "We really need to get it out of here."

"It's up to her," Gregory said. "She's the expert."

"Yes, then. Definitely. The tone is fantastic."

Soon they were on their way home.

"So much for the big city," Gregory said. "I like La Grande, but it's too busy for me. Joseph is just the right size. It has a good feel to it."

"I couldn't agree more," Laura said.

The ride back was spent in silence, both deep in their own thoughts.

Gregory was arguing with himself that he had to be sensible and listen to his head, not his heart. Laura had made it perfectly clear when she arrived that she was not in the market for marriage. No, he would look Beth Marie up instead. That would help get rid of the ache he felt in his heart.

Laura was acutely aware of the man beside her, wishing he weren't so hooked on an old sweetheart. There were so many things she liked about him, but it was foolish to even think about it. Besides, she was determined not to marry.

They made no stops and soon reached Joseph with five minutes to spare.

seventeen

The computer, a gift from the congregation last Christmas, sat
on Gregory's desk, often silent and blank. He still preferred to
write out his sermon notes in longhand. Someday he might
use the keyboard as he wrote, but he was such a poor typist
that it took forever to type one line. He'd thought of dictating,
but that seemed awkward as well.

The boys used the computer far more than he did. On
Saturdays they took turns playing the games. He never
minded that they used it that one day. He wished he had Joel's
expertise with electronics, specifically computers. E-mail had
been a boon. How he enjoyed corresponding with other ministers and a few old friends. Now he would search for one he
had loved so long ago.

The morning after the trip to La Grande, Gregory asked
one of the computer specialists in Joseph to help him put out
a request to find Beth Marie. Fortunately he remembered her
married name was Ollinger.

"This an old friend, Pastor?"

"You could say that. I never thought about looking on the
Internet until Laura, our pianist, mentioned it yesterday."

"The electronic age is amazing, isn't it?" He leaned back
and pointed to the name on the screen with Beth Marie's
E-mail address. "There it is. Hasn't changed her name. You're
in luck."

Gregory shook his head in amazement. He was so behind
with things. He felt he was back in the Pony Express age.

"Couldn't your sons help you here?"

Gregory suddenly felt uncomfortable knowing Joel might

127

see a letter. When he had received the computer, he had been assured that certain controls were in place that would prevent his sons from accidentally wandering onto web sites that were unfit for young people to view, so he didn't have to worry about their going online if they wanted to. As far as he knew, Joel didn't go online, but he wasn't sure.

"Of course, they could help, but they're busy with sports, music, school, you name it."

"Sure. Well, that's it, Reverend."

After the technician left, Gregory composed his letter. He might say no more than *Hello, how are you?* He just had to hear, find out if she was doing okay, and ask her how things were going in the little town of Shelburne. He hadn't been back there since his mother's funeral.

He'd tried to forget Beth Marie. He had buried the year-books, photos, and letters she'd written the first year he was away at college deep in his footlocker. Nobody ever bothered it, least of all him. To throw away the memories was unthinkable; but for all he knew, the paper might have turned to dust by now.

Gregory knew it wasn't right to pine away for someone he could not have. *Thou shalt not covet* came to mind many times over the years. He'd preached on the subject once, but only once. It was too close to home; yet he knew God directed His ministers to preach on that which they, too, could learn from.

He thought of Joel, so like himself. All seriousness in his mind, all legs as his body was going through a growth spurt. Joel never spoke what was in his heart. When Gregory suggested he take up trumpet for the school band, his son had agreed. He had never said he preferred another instrument. Perhaps he didn't, yet perhaps he did.

Caleb was a different child altogether. He kept nothing in, voicing his disapproval on a variety of subjects. He would take piano lessons, but only because his mother had played the piano. Yes, he was his own person. He loved God and it was evident in his exuberant approach to others. He was an ideal child in many ways, but exasperating as well. Gregory knew he need never worry about his younger son. He would make his way in this world.

Well, now no longer married, having been widowed for nine years, he didn't think it inappropriate to make this search for Beth Marie.

≥

The answer came back with astonishing swiftness the morning after Gregory had made the request. Yes, there was a Beth Marie Ollinger living in Shelburne. An address and phone number were sent and he felt his heart pounding as he looked at the number and address. Could he really be in touch with her in a matter of minutes? And when he heard her voice, what then?

He decided to wait a day, maybe two, before dialing the number. He had to rehearse what he might say. He'd start off slow, ask how she'd been, how many children she had, things all women like to talk about. He might see if she wanted to keep in touch through E-mail. That could be fun.

Nobody knew about his search, though Laura was the one who had first suggested it. Should he tell her when he made contact, or should he just keep it to himself?

≥

Gregory wasn't prepared for the face that flashed on the screen above her words when he downloaded her message the following morning. He printed it out on the Desk Jet, then held the page in his hand. It was Beth Marie. He'd have recognized that smile anywhere.

Then he saw the salutation: *Grego!* Gregory winced at the memory of her pet name for him. He continued:

> *How many times have I thought about you over the years, wondering if I'd made the biggest mistake of my life?*
>
> *There you are in a small town, making a difference in people's lives. I'm so proud of you for going ahead with the ministry. You knew what you wanted and went after it in spite of obstacles.*
>
> *An irate client shot my husband two years ago. It was difficult, but I've managed to pick up the pieces and go on with things that interest me.*
>
> *I heard you were married, but your wife died, leaving you with two sons. How tragic for you.*

There was more, but he had to digest this first.

Beth Marie was a widow? Of course he'd hadn't heard because he hadn't kept in touch with anyone.

He sat with head down, letting the years pass before his mind. Holding her hand as they ran through the grass at the park. The hayride they'd taken one Halloween, the parties at church, the skating rink where they'd both learned to skate, falling on each other.

She would expect an answer, and as he sat, he thought about what he might say. How he was happy to hear from her, but sorry to hear about the death of her husband. He started typing.

I love the little town where I now preach. The people are genuine. True friends. And— He paused as Laura's face flashed through his mind. Why would he think of her now? Had she come to mean that much to him? No. Not hardly.

> *I wish I could send a photo of the boys and me, but I am not knowledgeable with these computers. Still learning. Now my Joel has no such problem. Almost thirteen. A good kid, but quiet.*

As he began writing about his sons, he realized how many

good things he had to say about his eldest. He paused. No sense in telling her everything in one letter. He'd save some for another day. He signed the letter *Love, Greg*. That seemed okay. It would let her know that he thought of her with more than a passing fondness.

Gregory shut down the computer, covered it, and slipped out of his office. He'd never thought he would be eager to read a letter, but he soon found himself hightailing it over to his office first thing each morning. The letters went back and forth all week long. Then one day the phone rang.

"Gregory Michael, is it really you? It's me. Beth Marie."

"Where are you?" he asked, his excitement mounting.

"At the Portland International Airport. I'm renting a car and driving to Joseph. I'm looking at a map as we speak."

eighteen

Gregory was stunned. Never had he dreamed of the possibility of Beth Marie coming here. They'd written back and forth the past week, but not once had she indicated anything about a visit. The idea had crossed his mind once, but he wasn't sure he was ready. It would take some getting used to. But now she was coming, just like that.

He had mixed emotions. One part of him was elated and could hardly wait to see her again. The other part wondered about the reaction of his congregation and the town—his sons—and Laura. He wasn't sure why Laura's face popped into his mind. So far, she was the only one who knew about Beth Marie. If it hadn't been for her suggestion, he would never have found Beth.

His next thought was of the house, but she wouldn't be staying there, so he put that worry out of his mind. He'd never hired a housekeeper, though he'd often thought about it. Then he thought about himself. He had changed a lot. He wasn't the tall, skinny, lean kid he'd been then, nor the shy kid, unsure of himself.

He also wondered about Beth Marie's soul. Had she found God? Did she serve Him? When they were kids, he hadn't thought it mattered, but now he knew it did, very much.

He reached for the phone just as Joel came into the study.

"Dad, who's Beth Marie?"

Gregory leaned forward, his heart giving a sudden lurch. "Beth Marie?"

"Yeah. I shouldn't have looked at your E-mail, but I did. She calls you Grego. Nobody ever calls you Grego, or just Greg."

Gregory stared at his eldest son. "You're right. You invaded my privacy and I don't appreciate it. In answer to the second question, I never thought Greg sounded right for a preacher."

"So, who is Beth Marie?" Joel asked again.

"We grew up in the same town, but I haven't seen her for years." He cleared his throat. "She's coming for a visit."

"Here? In Joseph? From North Dakota?"

"Does that sound preposterous?"

"Yes, Dad, it does."

"Why?"

"Well, I just—oh, I don't know. What does she look like, and when is she coming, anyway?"

Gregory dug the picture out of his desk. "This came the other day. And she should be here by nightfall. She's renting a car in Portland."

"That soon?" Joel held the picture close. "She looks younger than you."

"And so she is, by at least two years. No, I think it's three."

"Does Laura know she's coming?"

Gregory looked away. "I haven't seen her to tell her. And why do you object to a friend of mine coming for a visit?"

Joel looked pained. "I just don't want anything to change."

"And what makes you think things will change, Son?"

"Because they do. Just when you get used to something, it all changes."

"Laura will always care about you, if that's what you're thinking about."

"I know that, Dad. I wasn't exactly thinking about me."

"Oh, I see."

Joel finally left and Gregory sat staring into space. Had he made a bad choice? Would Beth Marie's coming change things? He contemplated that for a long moment. Like Joel, he didn't want things to change. For the first time in a long while, he'd felt a state of contentment.

He shook the thoughts from his mind and went over his sermon again, but he couldn't concentrate. Of course Laura would look at the notes Friday and make suggestions. He looked forward to sitting over the table in the fellowship hall while she penciled in comments, then asked if he agreed. He always did. She never changed his content, but her suggestions helped him present his ideas more forcefully. He had decided to preach from Hebrews, the faith chapter. He closed his Bible and paper-clipped his notes. This sermon might be short.

⋆

Ruth heard about Beth Marie from Joel, who wasted no time in coming over to tell her. She knew he had to talk to someone, and it was easier for him to tell her than Laura.

"Do you believe someone can fall in love with someone they loved as a kid?"

Ruth pondered that for a moment. "You know, Joel, that's a hard one. I suppose it happens. You read about it, hear about it happening, but people change so much. You know, you can't go back."

"I don't want her to come."

"Honey, it'll just be for a few days, probably. She must have a job back in North Dakota, a family there."

"Her husband died. I read Dad's E-mail."

"Joel! I can't believe you did that. Would you want someone to read your mail without asking?"

His face flushed. "No. I guess not. But there it was on E-mail, while I was looking for an answer from a kid in California. We're going to trade stamps."

After Joel left, it hit Ruth. She hadn't thought about Joel's feelings before. He loved Laura like a mother. He wanted no one to come along to upset everything. In his own mind, he had undoubtedly hoped that Laura and his father would fall in love and marry. She hoped her assessment was right, that this

Beth Marie would stay just a few days. Like Joel, she wanted nothing to happen between her pastor and this unknown woman.

Then it hit her again. It had been right here all along and she hadn't even noticed. Laura had fallen right into the mold, the one God had meant for her to fit into. She was the perfect wife for Gregory Michael Hall, the ideal mother for his two young sons. And Gregory loved her and she cared for him, though neither realized it yet.

Ruth finished ironing the kitchen curtains. She felt smug. Like a child with a secret. Far be it from her to say anything, but she'd do her best to see that this Beth Marie didn't stay long.

The phone rang. It was Gregory.

"Pastor, how are you doing today?"

There was a long silence. "Ruth, you'll never believe this, but I just found an old friend on the Internet and she's decided to come to Joseph for a visit."

"That right?" It was difficult to act surprised sometimes.

"Do you suppose she could have Laura's old room? I am sure it would suit my friend just fine."

"For how long, Gregory?"

Another long pause. "She didn't say, but I'm sure she won't be here long. She just wants to see me."

"And she's widowed?"

"Why, yes, how did you know that?"

"A good guess." Ruth seldom lied, but she didn't want to betray Joel's confidence. "Of course I'll have the room ready and waiting. When is she arriving?"

"Sometime this evening."

"Today?"

"Well, yes, she flew into Portland. She's driving over."

"The beds are always clean, the floors are always vacuumed. No problem."

"Thanks, Ruth."

ҙ҇

Laura didn't know about Beth Marie Ollinger's arrival, as she had taken one of her elderly patients to the town of Wallowa for a niece's birthday. They had ended up staying the night as a windstorm blew in and the patient wanted to stay.

When Laura arrived back at her cottage, she saw the light blinking on the phone.

It was Gregory. "Laura! I wanted you to be the first to know. Remember I told you Beth Marie had contacted me? I have you to thank for that, and now she's coming—tonight! I want you to meet her whenever you can break away from your busy schedule."

There was a second message, this time from Joel. "Laura, I need to talk to you."

Laura was sorry she hadn't been here for Joel yesterday. It was now eleven. She usually met Gregory at church to go over his sermon. Would he be there today, or would he and Beth Marie be off sight-seeing?

She called the house. Nobody home. She called Ruth to see if she knew anything.

"My dear, where have you been?"

She explained, then asked about the newcomer to town.

"Beth Marie is staying here. In your old room."

"How long?"

"My heavens, everyone wants to know that. Gregory said just a few days, but I'm not sure. From the looks of things, she's here to stay!"

"Really?" Laura wasn't sure why, but she felt a sinking sensation in her midsection.

"Not to worry. She's the take-charge type. I thought she might be a clinging vine, but not this woman. She's a Martha Stewart if I ever saw one."

Laura giggled. Somehow she couldn't imagine a Martha Stewart in Joseph. Then she thought of Joel. She also couldn't imagine a Martha Stewart type as his new mother, either. Caleb could adjust, as he always did, but Joel would resist.

"I'll stop over to meet Beth Marie soon."

❧

Laura went over to church for a lesson at three. There was no sign of Gregory, nor was his sermon on top of the piano where he often put it. Distracted, she didn't even notice when Sarah hit some wrong notes.

"Mrs. Madison, aren't you going to scold me for so many mistakes?"

"What? Oh, Sarah, I think my mind wandered. Let's go over it again."

When Laura left after the second lesson, she stopped off at Ruth's. "No sign of them?"

"No. I think they went over to Pendleton and through the Pass to show there is still snow up there, even in the summer."

Laura was home, curled up with a book, when her phone rang. "They're back. It's kind of late, but why not come in the morning and you can meet her at breakfast."

"It's a deal," Laura said. "How about eight?" She knew that was the time Ruth served breakfast to her guests.

"No. Better make it at seven."

"Seven! That early?"

Ruth sighed. "Yes, seems they have another full day of sight-seeing planned."

"Are the boys going?"

"Of course. Gregory insists that it would be rude to do otherwise."

"How is Joel doing? He called here, but I couldn't get in touch with him."

"I don't know how she is with them, but here she chatters constantly. She's been everywhere, knows everything, and is rather—shall we say—opinionated?"

"Well, I guess Joel will survive."

"I hope so," Ruth said.

After hanging up, Laura wondered why the thought of Beth Marie upset her so. Of course it was because of the boys. Their welfare was important to her.

She opened her Bible and read an underlined passage, something she had marked years ago, 1 Corinthians 4:5: "Therefore judge nothing before the appointed time; wait till the Lord comes. He will bring to light what is hidden in darkness and will expose the motives of men's hearts. At that time each will receive his praise from God."

Laura read the passage twice, closed her Bible, and burst into tears. Later she admonished herself, not knowing why she reacted this way to God's word—or was it to Ruth's news? She wasn't quite sure which.

nineteen

Beth Marie was up and bustling around in the kitchen when Laura arrived the following morning.

"My dear, you have no idea how happy I am to meet you!" She threw her arms around Laura and gave her a tight hug. "All I've heard about since arriving is 'Laura this' and 'Laura that'—from the boys, you know."

Laura stepped aside and studied the woman before her. She was tall and graceful, not one pound overweight. Her long hair was pulled back and tied with a ribbon, she looked like she belonged on a farm. A white, frilly apron covered a fancy turquoise blouse and black slacks. Sensible shoes with block heels completed her attire.

"I've heard a lot about you, too," Laura replied.

Beth Marie handed her a cup of coffee. "This is decaf, you know. I brought my own special herbs and teas to cook with. So much of the stuff we eat is just plain no good for you."

"I really need caffeine," Laura started to protest, but Beth Marie rattled on.

"You'll get used to living without that horrible caffeine. Anyway," she continued, while opening the oven door and taking a peek, "I'm making my special wheat germ muffins— I can't thank you enough for suggesting that Greg find me on the Internet. I don't know why I hadn't thought of it before. Of course, I thought he'd be happily settled with wife number two and all."

She set the muffins in a bowl lined with a white linen cloth. "I know you'll adore these muffins. I told Ruth we can't have bacon or ham anymore. Turkey bacon is what I cook at home."

Ruth entered the kitchen and met Laura's gaze over Beth Marie's head. "Morning," she said, not as cheerfully as usual.

"I have never had—"

"Never had turkey bacon? Oh, my dear, it's simply wonderful stuff. I also brought my special nonfat cheese, and—well, you'll see."

Laura had a simple breakfast of decaffeinated coffee, special beans grown someplace she'd never heard of, muffins without butter, and tasteless eggs that were not eggs after all. She'd have to go home to find a real breakfast.

Ruth left half of her eggs on the plate, but that didn't faze Beth Marie.

"My dear, you have the right idea. Always leave food on the plate. We Americans eat far too much as it is."

After thirty minutes, Laura had a headache from the endless chatter. Soon she knew every last, minute detail of yesterday's excursion and how "divine" Gregory was for taking her. How "marvelous" the boys were, and how she looked forward to attending church and maybe even playing the piano for one of the services.

"Laura is our pianist," Ruth interrupted. "Perhaps you can play a special number for the offertory."

Beth Marie looked as if someone had slapped her. "Greg told me I could play perhaps next Sunday, but not this one, since Laura would have practiced the music for this week."

Laura said she had to go home; she had lessons to plan.

"That's quite all right, dear. I'll be leaving by 8:30, anyway. Greg is picking me up then; he's such an absolute dear."

❧

Laura kept busy the next few days. The July heat penetrated her skin. Sometimes she missed the cool ocean breeze. She had not once considered going back to Sealand, though Renee wrote every other week asking when she was returning. Then there was Kurt. Kurt with his complaints. She wondered now if she'd spoiled him by taking his side against Jerry. Maybe Jerry hadn't been too hard on him. He had tried to lead his family with the authority that was rightfully his as head of his household. Laura should have left well enough alone.

She sat on her back porch with its view to the mountain range, feet up, while staring at a blank sheet of paper. Beth Marie's words hit her as she tried to write to Renee. The woman unnerved her. She couldn't imagine Gregory being happy with this chatterbox, but how could she question him?

The phone rang and she jumped. It was Ruth.

"I need your help, hon, if you can spare me a few hours."

"What's wrong? You sound agitated. Are you sick?"

"Not sick. Not really. It's just that things are in an uproar here."

"You mean because of Beth Marie?"

Ruth laughed. "Isn't she something else?"

"Not quite what I expected."

"Me either. Me either, dear."

"So? What are you planning?"

"Going to visit my sister for a week or so."

"Now? During the tourist season?"

"Well, I have Miss Efficiency here, so why not take advantage of it? My sis, Molly, hasn't been well, as I may have mentioned to you. Seems she needs me to come."

"Well, Ruth, by all means go. I can help out there. You know I know what to do."

"Yes, but what about Beth Marie?"

Laura laughed. "Well, the turkey bacon definitely has to go. Do you think people are going to like that?"

"That's what worries me."

"Still no word as to how long she plans on staying?"

"Like I told you before, I think this is no mini-vacation. This woman has plans. We used to call them designs."

Laura put her writing supplies away. The letter to Renee could wait. "I'll be right over. We can plan while she's gone."

"Good girl. That's what I had in mind."

Laura hurried over the two blocks and entered the house without knocking.

Ruth poured them both a cup of tea and handed Laura a piece of sliced lemon, though she knew Laura didn't put lemon in her tea. Tears rolled, unchecked, down Ruth's cheeks.

"Ruth! What is it?"

"I didn't want to say this on the phone, but Molly got the results from some tests. It's cancer. That's why I must go to be with her."

"Ruth, I'm so sorry to hear this." Molly was the only family Ruth had left. Of course she'd want to be with her.

"I'll stay as long as you need me, and somehow I'll get along with Beth Marie."

Ruth squeezed more lemon into her tea. "Guess she'll have her wish for playing the piano on Sunday since the bed-and-breakfast keeps pretty busy and people are just starting to leave by eleven."

Laura touched the older woman's arm. "Ruth, that tea is going to be so sour you'll have to use half a cup of sugar to sweeten it."

"Oh." She laid the spoon in the saucer. "He's making a colossal mistake. Why are men so dumb when it comes to affairs of the heart?"

Laura felt a twinge. "He is a grown man, after all. Have you told him about Molly?"

"He, Beth Marie, and Caleb left before the call came."

"What about Joel?"

"He didn't go. Have no idea why."

"Should I take you over to Enterprise so you can leave today?"

"If you wouldn't mind."

"Of course not. Go pack."

On the way back from Enterprise, Laura wondered if Joel was home. On a hunch, she dropped off for her tennis shoes and decided to hike up the hill to the school. The bed-and-breakfast would be okay unattended for an hour.

Brisk walks never failed to calm her spirit when she felt downhearted, and she never tired of the view from the school, the mountains to the east, the smell of fresh mountain air.

She saw a form hunched over the guardrail, arms folded across his chest. Joel.

"Joel," she said his name softly. He didn't move. She could go away and not bother him, but she knew he knew she was there and not to say something seemed rude.

"Joel," she repeated.

He looked in her direction, and she noticed his eyes were red-rimmed. "Are you okay?" was all she could think of to ask.

He nodded, turning back to the view.

"I won't bother you. Just out walking myself."

"No, it's okay. I like talking to you."

Her heart warmed at his words. "And I like listening." She had to be careful and not say too much or too little. She'd wait and let him begin the topic for conversation.

"I don't like her being here."

"You mean Beth Marie?"

"Yeah. She talks constantly. Hangs onto Dad as if she'll never let go. He acts stupid. Doesn't he see how she is?"

"They were very good friends once."

"I know all that. I read some letters."

Laura understood Joel's reaction. He didn't understand that adults had feelings just like kids, that their feelings of love and caring and needing each other never quite went away.

"He doesn't even care about me and Caleb. He's just there for her."

"What if she were to become your mother?"

"No way!" Joel clenched his fists. "I'd run away. For sure."

"It takes time to know someone."

"I don't want to get to know her. She's—" he fished for an appropriate word— "idiotic!"

Laura stepped up to the guardrail and bent down, looking out over the valley. "What do you think you should do?"

Joel flexed his hands. "I guess that's why I'm talking to you."

Laura was trapped. What could she say to this hurting boy who never felt he measured up to his younger brother, who never felt good enough or that he did the right things for his father? Inside, he was softhearted. He just didn't know how to show his tender side. She wanted to reach over, to move the lock of hair that fell over one eye. She wanted to tell him that she ached for his pain as if it were her own. And, in essence, it actually was.

"I have no answers, Joel. God has the answer you need. You know He never gives us more burden than we can bear, nor does He close a window without opening another."

"I don't believe that."

"I don't think you mean that."

"You love my dad."

Laura jerked up. "What?"

"I can tell."

"Joel, I'm fond of him, but there's never been any feeling like that between us."

"Yeah, sure."

"You're mistaken." But even as she said the words, she felt the tugging deep inside her. She cared a lot more than she'd allowed herself to think or believe.

"He loves you, too, but doesn't know it."

"Joel, you can't know that."

"I watch him watching you."

Her cheeks flushed at the thought. "He admires my piano playing."

Joel shook his head. "It's more than that."

They both walked down the hill together as Laura tried to explain how things weren't always as they seemed. Somehow, she didn't think she'd convinced Joel. When they reached Ruth's, he headed for home while she hurried in to see if there were any messages.

❧

It was dark when Laura heard a car pulling up and voices in the evening air. She'd been sitting in her favorite chair, mulling over what Joel had said, wondering why her head said one thing and her heart another. She couldn't love Gregory Hall. She'd never planned on loving anyone again.

"You must come in, Greg," Beth Marie's voice called out. "I'll fix you some of my special hot chocolate. It's great! No fat. No sugar."

"And no taste," Laura said under her breath. She set her book down and rose.

Gregory murmured something that Laura couldn't quite hear.

The kitchen light came on, and it was then that Gregory saw her.

"Laura! What are you doing here?"

Gregory walked over, and Laura felt short of breath at the sight of him. "Ruth's gone to her sister's in Portland. Emergency."

"Oh, no. What happened?"

Laura handed him the letter. "It's all in here."

"My dear, that means you and I must run this bed-and-breakfast," Beth Marie interjected. A smile erupted. She wore a darling two-piece denim outfit, looking perfectly at home in this country. Her eyes shone as she looked from Laura to Gregory and back to Laura again.

"I'll tend to things here, and you can play piano for the services," Laura said.

Beth Marie's eyes grew even wider. "Oh, Greg, that's what

I really wanted to do, so you could see how I play and how things could—well, work out!"

Laura could hardly believe it. Talk about brazen! She was moving in lock, stock, and barrel, no doubt about it.

"I guess that'll work," Gregory said. "If it's okay with you, Laura. Laura?"

She knew he was looking at her, waiting for an answer, but Beth Marie answered before Laura could.

"I'll be here to help with the breakfast. That's plenty of time. Oh, this is so exciting!" She clasped her hands.

"That's okay," Laura managed. "You should maybe go over the hymns."

"Hymns?" Beth Marie turned around so quickly, she nearly dropped the teakettle. "Don't you ever play newer songs, Greg?"

Gregory looked almost chagrined. "The people here like the old hymns best. Of course, we can use a newer piece of music once in a while."

"Well, I hate those stuffy old slow hymns. I just know they'll love the songs I know."

Laura excused herself and went down the hall to Ruth's small bedroom, where she'd sleep. Laura got a lump in her throat as she thought about Ruth. It was strange to be here in this room, among her possessions. She looked at the huge doll collection around the room. She hadn't realized Ruth collected dolls. They were on shelves, little tables, rocking chairs. Everywhere. They were beautiful and unique. She'd have to suggest that Ruth put them somewhere so that guests could enjoy them.

She pulled back the quilt and tears came to her eyes as she felt Ruth's worry and concern over Molly. She wanted to have a prayer time, but Beth Marie's voice carried through the walls, so her room was not quiet. She couldn't help wondering what would happen in church on Sunday when Beth

Marie insisted on playing the songs she liked. She had an idea it wouldn't matter what Gregory said. Beth Marie would have her way.

O Lord, help us all, she prayed, finally drifting off to the sound of the younger woman's voice going on and on.

twenty

The days turned into one week, then two, and Laura found it difficult to work with Beth Marie, who felt she was right and wanted everything her way. Kenny Thompson stopped by one day, and Laura chuckled as it looked as if he'd met his match in the talking department.

"Goodness, but that man can talk," Beth Marie said after he left.

She was dressed in a skirt and blouse with a frilly apron around her waist, and Laura had noticed Kenny watching Beth's every move.

"I understand you've dated him."

Laura shrugged. "Yes, but I'm not interested."

"He has money."

"Money isn't everything."

Laura had baked chocolate chip cookies for Caleb because he seemed down at his last lesson. Even having his own piano hadn't cheered him up. Joel also came by periodically and they talked or played Scrabble when Laura wasn't busy cooking, cleaning rooms, or doing laundry. Beth Marie liked the cooking part, not the cleaning.

Laura started planning on a trip to the beach for after Ruth's return. She needed to get away to think, and Ruth was due back soon. She called almost every day to see how things were.

"Molly's doing so much better and urges me to go home," she'd said recently.

"We all miss you, you must know that," Laura responded.

❧

The day before Ruth was due back, Renee called. It was past

midnight, Laura noticed on her lighted digital. Shivering, she groped for her robe and made her way to the phone. Ruth, bless her heart, did not believe in portable phones, nor was there an extension in her bedroom.

Shivering, Laura grabbed her robe. Who would call this time of night? Emergency. It had to be. Her mind flitted to the possibilities. One of her kids. The house had burned. Renee was in an accident. . .

"Laura, can you come? Kurt's in the hospital—"

"Hospital!"

"He was coherent enough to think to tell the doctor to call me since he couldn't remember your phone number."

"But what happened? An accident?"

"No, it's some sort of crazy high fever. I just spoke with the doctor."

Laura shivered again, panic threading through her. "What's the prognosis?" She remembered another time, a trip overnight to the hospital when Kurt raged with fever. He seemed to run one at the first sign of illness. The other two had not.

"They're taking tests."

"I'm sitting the bed-and-breakfast, but there's someone who can take over." Beth Marie could handle it just fine. "I'll leave just as soon as I can pack a couple of things."

"And don't worry and drive like a madwoman," Renee said, knowing Laura's inclination to drive fast anyway. "We want you to arrive in one piece. He'll be okay."

"Nobody can be sure about anything except that God makes the world turn. And we can be certain of His love for us."

❧

"Guess this is the end of your sight-seeing tours," Laura said to a yawning Beth Marie, who was walking down the stairs. Of course, she was wearing an elegant frothy pink robe and matching scuffs. "I have to leave. My son's in the hospital." She handed Beth Marie a number. "Just in case you need help."

Beth Marie drew herself up. "Honey, I'm not worried about running this place. It's too bad about your kid."

"Yes, well, these things happen."

"You don't like me, do you?" Beth Marie followed Laura back to her room.

"What makes you think that?"

"I just know. I feel it."

Laura grabbed her suitcase from under the bed. "I'm sorry if I gave that impression."

"I love Greg, you know," Beth Marie said, stepping aside as Laura started throwing clothes in her suitcase, "and I intend to do everything to win him over."

Laura nodded. "That's fair enough. He's been alone a long time and needs someone." Even as she said it, a sudden feeling of loss hit her, one she couldn't quite explain.

"Needs?" Beth Marie scoffed. "Not hardly. How about all those people in his congregation?"

"That's different. He needs a special someone—a wife. All men of the cloth do."

"They have God."

"Yes, of course, but someone tangible is also nice. You've undoubtedly heard of the saying, 'You can be in a room full of people and feel alone'?"

"No, can't say that I have." Beth Marie studied her fingernails as if that was the most important thing in her life.

"Well, if you'll excuse me, I must dress. But rest assured I wish you a world of happiness."

"And I hope your son will be all right."

"Thanks," Laura said as she closed the door. If she didn't, she had a feeling Beth Marie would stand there all morning discussing her needs.

Ten minutes later, Laura grabbed the coffee Beth Marie offered, even if it was decaf.

"And take one of my muffins. It'll fill you up."

"I think I'd like some of the cinnamon toast, too."

Beth Marie wrinkled her nose. "You mean that dry stuff in the box?"

"Yep. It's good. Try it sometime."

Without waiting for a comment, Laura hurried out the door, hopped in her car, fastened the belt, and nosed her car out of the driveway. Why had she gotten into a discussion with Beth Marie this morning of all times? Beth Marie was right. Laura didn't like her much. And she didn't think Beth Marie was what Gregory needed. A tremor ran up her spine as she thought of that afternoon when he'd kissed her forehead. Silly for her to think of that now.

One thing she knew for certain: She couldn't leave without at least leaving Gregory a note about the situation. She swallowed hard. She couldn't go to the house. She didn't want to talk to him face-to-face. She regretted not being able to tell the boys good-bye, but she'd send an E-mail to Joel and a note to Caleb. They'd understand an emergency. Of course, they'd all manage nicely. Why did she think not? Then she remembered Joel that afternoon at the school and his pinched face.

Laura drove to the church, dashed off a line about the phone call, giving few details because she didn't have them anyway. She put the note under the door. Gregory would find it when he came to work on his sermon later this morning. He always worked early, but since Beth Marie had come, his hours were jumbled up and she never quite knew what he was doing or where he was. He'd changed practically overnight to a person who had no schedules, no rules.

The door sprang open as she hurried down the steps. "And what is this? Since when do you go around putting notes under doors?"

Laura stopped without turning. She knew how Gregory would look, his blue eyes with questions in them, a hand raking through his hair, the tilt of his head. Now that she thought about it, leaving a note did seem like something a schoolgirl would do.

She turned and glanced up, her eyes not quite meeting his gaze. "I didn't really think you would be here. I am leaving for Sealand. Kurt's in the hospital. I know nothing more than the note says."

Gregory opened the slip of paper. "Laura?"

"Yes?" Why was she acting this way? Since when could she not look him in the eye? Suddenly and unexpectedly, tears filled her eyes. "I really didn't want to talk to you." There. She'd finally said it.

He came down the steps and took her hand. "Has it come to that? That we can't talk? That I can't take time to pray for your son, your trip?"

She turned and looked up into his craggy face. "I suppose it has."

"Will you be gone long?"

"I haven't a clue. It's just that I'm needed there and not here."

"Who says we don't need you here?"

"Gregory, I never promised to stay. It was a dream to fulfill, something I wanted to do. I had to get away from the beach and all the memories. Surely you, above all people, can understand that."

There was that word "need." Funny how she had used it twice already today. She supposed everyone needed someone, but she'd tried to believe she was indispensable. Now her eldest son was ill and needed her.

It was time to face some important decisions. Gregory needed her in a different way, if in fact he needed her at all. It wasn't quite in the way she had hoped once, though even in the beginning she'd known it was impossible. Younger men didn't marry older women. It was always the other way around. Yet she knew that he found her attractive. From the first day there had been a magnetism, though they had argued on several occasions. Before Beth Marie, he seemed to hang on her every word, liked to hear her play, enjoyed her working over his sermons, and appreciated the way she could talk with Joel.

She waved the kind of half-wave one does when unsure. She wanted him to say something else. She had the urge to turn, to throw her arms around him, asking him if he really loved Beth Marie. But it wasn't to be.

Gregory didn't want her to leave—not yet. "Laura, don't go thinking you aren't needed here. Everyone will miss you. Surely you realize that."

He longed to go after her, stop her on the steps, take her in his arms. The thought seemed to shatter inside him, moving through his extremities. What was this? He was thinking about Laura in a way he'd never let himself come to grips with.

But what about Beth Marie? She was here now. His dream had always been that one day they would be together again. Why, then, did Laura's face keep getting in the way? Was she coming back? He really needed to know that. But of course she probably didn't know. He knew her son had wanted her to return since she'd first come. How dire was the emergency?

She choked back tears that threatened. "I'll miss the boys. Please tell them I'll be in touch."

Without another word, her hand left the railing. "I hope you and Beth Marie will truly be happy."

He watched her walk away. As she rounded the corner of the church, he moved to the last step so he could see her get into her car, back out, and head down the street toward town. He waved, but he didn't think she waved back.

A funny, hollow feeling came over him. Why hadn't he held her for just a moment? She'd looked so vulnerable, so in need of being held. Why hadn't he been able to go after her?

The idea was preposterous. She couldn't possibly have any feelings for him. Yet there had been a look on her face when their gaze had met and held, a fierce intensity, yet sweet concern.

Gregory felt his heart sink. *Lord, I'm not reading this right. My life is in more of a shambles than before. How could this happen?* The sun beat down and warmed him on the outside, but his insides felt suddenly cold.

He had a sermon to prepare and dinner with Beth Marie. Knowing her, she'd come around before that and talk about something. She always found something to talk about.

He sighed. Laura's face came to mind again. Why had he not realized how much she had come to mean to him? *God, go with her. Give her peace in her heart. Heal her boy.*

At that, he thought of his own son Joel. She had touched Joel's life and meant so much to him, and Gregory was suddenly worried about him.

twenty-one

Laura's tears fell as she drove out of Joseph. Thank heavens for the box of tissues she kept in the front seat. She dabbed her cheeks, chiding herself for getting involved. *Lord, I asked for a mission of sorts. You gave it to me, as I knew You would, but why did You let someone else come in and reap the benefits? Is Beth Marie the right woman for Gregory? The right mother for those precious sons?*

At the thought of her own son, the tears started again. It was a good thing she'd become familiar with the road, also good that it was early enough so the road was empty. Kurt had wanted her to come home, and so she was. Home, where she was also needed. But Joseph seemed like home now.

The sunrise was gorgeous, and she cried again at God's infinite beauty. *O Lord, I'm just being an emotional, middle-aged woman. I don't know what I want, so You're settling it for me, making my decisions.* Yet she knew that, though God was in charge of her life, decisions were hers alone to make. Hadn't He let Adam and Eve make mistakes when He could have stopped them?

She stopped once for gas, but pushed on, arriving in Sealand in the middle of the afternoon. The drive across the bridge had made her cry again. She hoped her eyes wouldn't be puffy by the time she reached the hospital. Kurt didn't need to see her like this.

❧

Laura stayed at Kurt's side all night. His fever raged, and she dabbed his forehead with a cool cloth. Nurses came in and checked his vital signs on the hour. She was so grateful for their concern.

Renee had come and gone. Hugging, they had clung to each other.

"I missed you so much, but I sure didn't want something like this to bring you back."

"Me neither."

Renee studied her face. "You look thinner."

"I guess I haven't been eating any of your delicious scones."

"Yeah, sure. It's that preacher, isn't it?"

"Not hardly."

"Well, say what you will, but I wasn't born yesterday."

❧

Pastor Dave and a few other friends came. Everyone prayed with her as she stood vigil. Now she was alone with Kurt, and all she could do was pray and sponge off his face. She felt so helpless. She wondered about Mary and how helpless she must have felt about Jesus, knowing there was nothing she could do to change the course of His life.

What sort of infection is this? Why doesn't it react to any of the medications? Tubes dripped into Kurt, offering him sustenance.

A nurse appeared in the doorway. "Why don't you go home, Mrs. Madison? We can call you if there is a change. You need some sleep."

Home. Laura felt a sudden jolt. *Home.* Exactly where was home?

"I'll stay, if you don't mind."

"Of course." She swished from the room, and Laura stared at the closed door. She reached up and grabbed Kurt's hand. *Oh, please, God, don't take my eldest child from me. I don't know if I can bear it.*

She slipped into a fitful sleep and was slumped over the bed, her hand still holding Kurt's, when Dr. Gleason entered the room.

"I'm surprised to see you still here."

"I couldn't leave him. I'm all he has. His dad—" she choked—"his father was in a boating accident four years ago."

He touched her shoulder. "I remember, Laura."

"Doctor, what if his fever doesn't go down? Will he be brain-dead?"

"The next twenty-four hours are crucial."

"Have you taken all the tests?"

"We're waiting for the results of a spinal tap now."

"When will you know?"

"Soon, I hope. Now, why not go get something to eat? You're a wreck. Do you want him to see you looking like this?"

Laura tried to smile. "No. You're right."

She left to grab a bite to eat from a local café. The hospital was too small to have a cafeteria. Evelyn, a friend she had been on the library board with, nodded from a far corner.

"Laura Madison, I haven't seen you forever." She motioned for Laura to share her table. "I hear you went off to the mountains."

"Yes, I've been in eastern Oregon for the past four months."

"Why there?"

Laura turned her cup upright and nodded when the waitress stood with the full pot in hand.

"It's a long story, but I needed a change."

"Oh."

"Now I'm back because my Kurt's in the hospital having tests."

After discussing the findings thus far and thanking her friend for her concern, Laura ordered a bowl of oatmeal. "With raisins, please."

"I'm sorry to hear about Kurt," continued Evelyn. "Are you moving back then?"

"I really don't know." The ache that had been in her heart

on the trip over suddenly returned. "I'm too shattered to make any decisions just now."

"Well, we can always use you around here."

Evelyn rose. "Speaking of meetings, I have to be at the museum in ten minutes, but it's been good to see you again." She hesitated. "I'll certainly pray for your son."

"Thanks."

Laura stirred sugar into her coffee though she never used sugar. She had to do something with her hands. Strange how life had changed for her. She'd been happy here at the coast for many years, yet now she wanted to return to the Wallowa area. But for what reason? Because she missed Joel and Caleb? The church? Playing the piano? Yes, of course. But it was much more. She missed a certain person who had taken up residence in her heart. How could she have let it happen? Could God have directed her path towards one Gregory Michael Hall? But Gregory didn't need her. He liked her, but he was in love with Beth Marie, a.k.a. superwoman.

The oatmeal came with brown sugar on top. "Would you like more coffee?" the waitress asked.

"Yes, that would be nice." She stared at the oatmeal and, though hungry, she doubted she could eat it.

God, Laura prayed for what seemed like the tenth time that morning, *help my son get well. And please help me to know what to do with my life. Give me purpose. Help me to understand. And, above all, help me to get Gregory out of my heart.*

Thy will be done flashed through Laura's mind. Of course she'd forgotten to add that. She forgot a lot of the time. She knew, as she'd always known, that He was there to help her overcome any and all fears. He would walk her along the path, carry her if need be. And He always answered prayers, though sometimes the answer was "No."

"I have to get back," she said when the waitress came, asking if she wanted anything more.

She walked the three blocks to the hospital, pulling her collar up around her neck. Mornings could be cold at the beach. A dampness penetrated her thin coat. It was August and one did not wear a coat in Joseph during this season.

The nurse met her at Kurt's door. "We have the test results back."

"You do? Oh, praise God!"

"The doctor will be with you in a minute."

"But he'll be all right?"

"The treatment has started."

Laura entered her son's room. His eyes were closed, but his face didn't feel as hot.

"Laura, good news!" Dr. Gleason exclaimed as he entered the room. "It's curable, though he's going to need rest."

"What is it, exactly?"

"He has adhesions on the spine. It caused numbness on his right side. With the medication and proper bed rest, he should be okay in a few weeks. Of course, this is a strange case. Usually a fever doesn't accompany this affliction."

Laura smiled. "My son has never had normal anything."

She called Renee to tell her the good news.

"No working for a few weeks, eh?"

"Knowing Kurt, he'll be back on his feet in less time than that."

Later that night, his eyes suddenly opened, lighting up when he saw her. "Mom! I thought I had a dream and you were here, holding my hand."

"It was no dream." She leaned over and kissed his cheek as tears filled her eyes. "I love you so very much, Son."

He held her hand in a tight grip. "What's wrong with me, anyway? I remember feeling woozy, numb, and then nothing."

"A friend found you at work and couldn't rouse you."

Kurt smiled. His face, now wan, looked hopeful. "I just wish Susan was here."

It was then Laura realized her son's girlfriend was missing. She didn't know why she hadn't thought of her before.

"Where *is* Susan?"

"She left. Went to Seattle to find a job."

"Honey, I had no idea."

"That was one reason I wanted you to come home, so you could talk to her or at least tell me what to do."

Laura took his hand. "Kurt, I can't make decisions for you now. It's up to you. If you want her back, maybe you have to go look for her. When you're on your feet again, of course."

"You're right. I guess I have this idea that you have the answer to everything, Mom."

"I don't, Kurt. I never have. It's God who can help you work through a problem, God who gives you a sense of direction. It's time you turned to Him."

Kurt was released the following morning to recuperate at home. Laura brought clean clothes from his apartment. "Just think. Your own bed again. Won't that be nice?"

twenty-two

Gregory was at loose ends and didn't know why. Joel was not speaking to him. Ruth seemed perturbed about something, his parishioners missed Laura's playing, and some said they missed her, period. Even Caleb was quiet.

Beth Marie had taken over. He wasn't sure how it had happened. One day he was completely enthralled with her, so glad they had met again; the next thing he knew, she had altered his sermon subjects and changed the music. The congregation was now singing all new tunes and the words were printed on the overhead. Many members were disgruntled at the sudden changes. Gregory feared a backlash. He decided to stop by and discuss the problem with Ruth. She was always a good listener.

Ruth looked thoughtful. "Are you asking me what you should do in the situation?"

Gregory shrugged. "I suppose you could say that."

"Why not come right out and tell Beth Marie you care for her as a friend? Women understand what that means."

"I don't know if Beth Marie would even hear me if I said that."

"I've got it!" Ruth claimed. "Kenny Thompson. Why not set up a date between the two of them?"

"He's met her—"

"And she him."

"But nothing has come of it."

"Doesn't mean it wouldn't work if we helped a little."

Gregory went home feeling better about the situation. He missed Laura like crazy, far more than he'd ever thought possible. He'd been calling the hospital each day to check on Kurt's condition but had refrained from asking for Laura. Still, he felt compelled to go see her in person. He wanted to see if she felt the same way. Now if that wasn't silly thinking!

He could close his eyes and see her smile, see the way her hair tossed in the wind, the warmth she passed on to everyone she met. She took the time to listen. She'd made Joel care about living. She'd brought them together as father and son.

Gregory got home to find Caleb watching cartoons.

"Where's Joel?"

"I don't know."

"Did he come home from his walk?"

Caleb shrugged. "Don't know, Dad."

He went up the stairs to the boys' bedrooms. Joel's was neat, the opposite of Caleb's. Joel had everything in place, and his desk was straightened with two books on top. Two pairs of shoes were side by side under the bed, no dirty clothes on the floor. A book was open to Shakespeare's *Macbeth*.

There was no note on the desk or bed or on the pad on the kitchen bulletin board.

When Joel didn't come home by seven, Gregory was concerned. Where could the kid be?

He finally got in the car and drove through town and out by Wallowa Lake. No sign of his son, nor had anyone seen him. He stopped at Ruth's again. She hadn't heard from Joel, either.

Where could he go? What stone had he left unturned? He prayed, which he should have done in the beginning. *God, help me to know where Joel is.*

Driving up the hill to the junior-senior high school gave him a funny feeling. With school out, the buses were parked in the garage, and an empty parking lot gave the whole area a look of abandonment. He saw Joel quite by accident, though he knew God had directed him there. Joel stood at the far end of the school grounds, looking out over the mountains. Hands in his pockets, he stared into space. He didn't even turn when Gregory walked over.

"Joel. Why are you here?"

Finally he looked at his father, his shoulders stiff, his body unyielding. "I always come here to think. So does Laura. And I don't want to talk about it."

"Don't or won't?"

"What's there to say?" He turned and Gregory saw the trace of tears on the young boy's face. He longed to go to him, to pull him close, and it was then as if a voice was directing him, saying, *Do it. If you feel love, show it.*

"Joel," he said again, reaching out his arms. Then the boy was there, and they clung to each other, tears intermingling.

"I had no idea you were in pain. I wish you could come to me."

"Dad, I miss Laura. I've tried to like Beth Marie. She told me how you two would have married if her mother hadn't interfered, and I know she loves you, but I don't like her."

It was a long speech for Joel.

"I don't love Beth Marie, Son."

"You don't?"

"I did at one time, and I thought I might rekindle what we once felt for each other, but it hasn't happened. Like you, I feel an intense loneliness for Laura. I want to bring her back. I want her to stay here in Joseph, be part of my life. Our life."

Joel's face split into a wide grin. "Dad, she'd do it, I know she would."

"How can you know? One never knows for sure."

"I do know. I just do, Dad. C'mon, we gotta go and bring her back."

That night Gregory called the hospital and was told Kurt had been released. The nurse refused him Kurt's home phone number, so he called information.

This phone call would be one of the most important calls

he'd made in his life, and God was behind his decision. He just knew it. He'd take it one step at a time. He and the boys would visit her at the coast and meet Kurt. They would talk.

But, before that could happen, his first step was to talk to Beth Marie.

❧

"But we belong together, Greg," Beth Marie said, a pout on her full, red lips. "You've always loved me. You said so yourself."

He looked at the woman in front of him. Not one hair out of place. Her long navy blue skirt reached the top of fancy leather boots. Her deep purple shirt was frilly. Her cheeks were rosy, but it was blusher, not natural. She was nothing like Laura.

"We've changed, Beth. I don't think we want the same things anymore."

"I can be a good minister's wife—"

He nodded. "Perhaps too good."

She laughed, throwing her arms around him. "How can anyone be too good?"

"Maybe 'good' isn't the right word. I just know it wouldn't work for us."

She left his home, holding her head high. "I'll change your mind. Just you wait and see."

"I doubt it," Gregory said under his breath.

❧

In the morning, Laura was making pudding, as Kurt's diet had to be light, when the phone rang. Kurt answered in his bedroom.

"Sure. I'm doing fine. Yes, my mom is here."

Laura grabbed the kitchen extension, certain it must be one of her friends who had learned she was back in town.

"Laura? How are you? And how is Kurt doing?"

Her heart lurched as she recognized the deep voice. "Gregory. And how are you?"

"I asked the first question."

She closed her eyes, visualizing his face, the thick thatch of hair. "Kurt needs plenty of rest and should be fine in a week or so."

"I called every morning to check on his condition."

"You did? But nobody told me."

"I know. I wanted it that way."

"How are Joel and Caleb?"

"Caleb says if you don't come back, he wants to sell the piano."

"Oh, sure." Her heart began pounding.

"So Kurt is going to be okay? Would you say the crisis has passed?"

"As far as I know." She wondered what his questions were leading to, but she wouldn't ask. "I'm staying with him for a few days until he gets on his feet again."

"I'm coming there. The boys, too."

"Coming here? But what about church?"

"A pastor over in Enterprise is filling in. His church has a special revival going on this week."

"But—"

"Don't you want us to come?"

Her heart lurched again. "I was just wondering about Beth Marie. Will she be along?"

"She's gone home."

"Home?"

"Yes, but she's coming back."

"I see."

"No, you don't, but I don't want to explain it on the phone. I want to see you in person. We'll be there tonight. Oh, and Ruth sends her love. Her sister's prognosis is good. They think they got all the cancer."

"That's terrific news. Give her my love, too."

"Must finish packing. And Caleb is wired. I may let him

run behind the car on the way."

Laura laughed, then said good-bye.

❧

When Gregory's car was packed, the boys climbed in, eager for a long ride to the coast. As they rode, Caleb kept saying over and over, "Dad, you mean you love Laura and she might be our mom?"

"I don't know, Caleb. We won't know until we get there."

❧

Kurt's eyes were on Laura when she came into his bedroom, bringing a bowl of pudding.

"So, Mom. What's going on? Your cheeks are pinker than I've ever seen them."

"Oh, Kurt. God answers prayers in the most unusual, wonderful ways, just as He will answer your prayer about Susan. I know He will."

"But what's going on?"

"You'll see. This evening. We just have to wait."

"Wait?"

"Wait for Gregory, Joel, and Caleb to arrive."

As Laura cleaned the kitchen, she knew she'd be counting the hours until Gregory Michael Hall and his two wonderful sons arrived.

twenty-three

They arrived that evening, tired, hungry, and "gritty" as Caleb put it.

Laura embraced first Caleb, then Joel, and gave a quick hug to Gregory.

"Hi, I'm Caleb!" said the boy, wasting no time in introducing himself to Kurt, who sat propped up on his couch.

"I've been hearing about you over the past few hours."

"Good things?" Gregory asked, extending his hand.

Laura watched as Kurt sized up the older man.

"All good things," Kurt said.

Laura thought Kurt's color had improved since he'd come home.

"Your mother and I have some unfinished business to discuss," Gregory said. "The boys know and have agreed to stay here and keep you company—if that's all right."

"Of course," Kurt said, looking from his mother back to the preacher.

He helped her on with a light jacket, and they took Laura's car as she headed for her favorite spot on the beach.

"This is, or used to be, my thinking place," she explained. It was dark, but a near-full moon shone down from a dark sky. They stayed in the car because it was warmer.

"I've done a lot of thinking. Praying. Talking to the boys."

"Yes?" She wondered if he could hear her heart beating.

"I love you, Laura. Plain and simple. I don't know how you feel about me, but I know you love the boys and they need you. I need you, but more important I want you to be part of my life, to share in my joys, my concerns, and just everything that comes to the Hall family." He took her hand and held it tight. "I don't expect you to answer now. You must be very sure. My heart would break should you change your mind down the road."

"And Beth Marie? What about her? How do you know you are over her?"

His expression changed. "I was foolish, carrying a torch all those years. I know God will forgive me, and I pray that others will, too."

"I'm sure they will if there's something to forgive."

"I suggested to Kenny Thompson that he might ask her out when she returns with her belongings."

Laura laughed. "Beth Marie is just the one to help run that ranch!"

"Yes, she is. And she can also play the piano on occasions such as. . .well, I was thinking about a honeymoon in Vancouver British Columbia, should a certain person say 'yes' to my proposal."

Tears filled Laura's eyes as she turned and lifted her face for his kiss. A real kiss, not just one from her dreams or a kiss on the forehead like that day in his office.

"I think that certain person would say 'yes' should she get a proposal from the right man."

"I don't have a ring."

"That can come later."

He kissed her again, noticing how the moonlight hit her hair, making it almost shine, but not nearly as much as her face.

"I think we should go back and make an announcement to our sons."

"Our sons," Laura repeated. "Yes, I like the sound of it."

"And I think we should offer a prayer of thanks to God, our Creator. I, for one, thank Him for a certain ad that appeared in the *Chieftain*."

"And I thank Him for your answering that ad." They bowed their heads and prayed.

Afterwards, Gregory asked, "Should we have a small wedding or invite the whole town?"

Laura giggled. "We may as well invite the whole town. We might even get as many people as the Chief Joseph Powwow! And I want Ruth to bake the cake and my friend Renee to be my matron of honor."

"Done!"

"Do you hear that?" Laura asked.

Gregory listened. "Hear what?"

"It's singing. I think angels are singing a happy melody in heaven."

Gregory took her hand again. "You should write books with that imagination," he said, and she couldn't help noticing the wide smile on his face, as the moonlight lit up the streaks of gray in his hair.

"Let's go back and see what happens."

As they passed the place where they'd found Jerry washed ashore, Laura felt a gentle regret surface, but she supposed that would always happen. This place and the things that had happened here were part of her. She'd be back. The beach would always be home to her, but now she was ready to return to Joseph and to the new life that beckoned.

Ruth's Rhubarb Custard Pie

Make a double crust and line a 9" pie pan with bottom crust.

Filling:
Beat 3 eggs slightly.
Add 3 tablespoons milk.
Mix and stir in:
2 cups sugar, ¼ cup flour, ¾ teaspoon nutmeg.
Wash, chop up (¼" chunks), and mix in 4 cups pink rhubarb.

Pour filling into pastry-lined pie pan.
Dot with 1 tablespoon butter.
Cover with top crust.
Bake until nicely browned. Make sure pie is bubbling.
Best when served slightly warm.

Temperature: 400°
Time: 50–60 minutes.

A Letter To Our Readers

Dear Reader:

In order that we might better contribute to your reading enjoyment, we would appreciate your taking a few minutes to respond to the following questions. We welcome your comments and read each form and letter we receive. When completed, please return to the following:

Rebecca Germany, Fiction Editor
Heartsong Presents
PO Box 719
Uhrichsville, Ohio 44683

1. Did you enjoy reading *A Tender Melody*?
   ☐ Very much. I would like to see more books by this author!
   ☐ Moderately
   I would have enjoyed it more if _____
   _____
   _____

2. Are you a member of **Heartsong Presents**? Yes ☐ No ☐
   If no, where did you purchase this book?_____
   _____

3. How would you rate, on a scale from 1 (poor) to 5 (superior), the cover design?_____

4. On a scale from 1 (poor) to 10 (superior), please rate the following elements.

   ____ Heroine   ____ Plot

   ____ Hero   ____ Inspirational theme

   ____ Setting   ____ Secondary characters

5. These characters were special because_____

   _____

   _____

6. How has this book inspired your life?_____

   _____

   _____

7. What settings would you like to see covered in future
   Heartsong Presents books?_____

   _____

   _____

8. What are some inspirational themes you would like to see
   treated in future books?_____

   _____

   _____

9. Would you be interested in reading other **Heartsong
   Presents** titles?   Yes ❑   No ❑

10. Please check your age range:
    ❑ Under 18   ❑ 18-24   ❑ 25-34
    ❑ 35-45   ❑ 46-55   ❑ Over 55

11. How many hours per week do you read?_____

Name _____

Occupation _____

Address _____

City _____ State _____ Zip _____

Experience the joy of love...

Romance readers will love this brand-new collection of contemporary inspirational novellas, all centered on the season of spring. Includes the stories *E-Love* by Gloria Brandt, *The Garden Plot* by Rebecca Germany, *Stormy Weather* by Tracie Peterson, and *Bride to Be* by Debra White Smith.

400 pages, Paperbound, 5 ³/₁₆" x 8"

·····Heart♥ng·····

CONTEMPORARY ROMANCE IS CHEAPER BY THE DOZEN!

Any 12
Heartsong
Presents titles
for only
$26.95 *

Buy any assortment of twelve *Heartsong Presents* titles and save 25% off of the already discounted price of $2.95 each!

*plus $1.00 shipping and handling per order
and sales tax where applicable.

HEARTSONG PRESENTS *TITLES AVAILABLE NOW:*

(If ordering from this page, please remember to include it with the order form.)

·····Presents·····

Great Inspirational Romance at a Great Price!

Heartsong Presents books are inspirational romances in contemporary and historical settings, designed to give you an enjoyable, spirit-lifting reading experience. You can choose wonderfully written titles from some of today's best authors like Veda Boyd Jones, Yvonne Lehman, Tracie Peterson, Debra White Smith, and many others.

When ordering quantities less than twelve, above titles are $2.95 each.
Not all titles may be available at time of order.

SEND TO: **Heartsong Presents** Reader's Service
P.O. Box 719, Uhrichsville, Ohio 44683

Please send me the items checked above. I am enclosing $_____
(please add $1.00 to cover postage per order. OH add 6.25% tax. NJ add 6%.). Send check or money order, no cash or C.O.D.s, please.
To place a credit card order, call 1-800-847-8270.

NAME _____

ADDRESS _____

CITY/STATE _____ ZIP _____

HPS 5-99

Hearts♥ng Presents

Love Stories Are Rated G!

That's for godly, gratifying, and of course, great! If you love a thrilling love story, but don't appreciate the sordidness of some popular paperback romances, **Heartsong Presents** is for you. In fact, **Heartsong Presents** is the *only inspirational romance book club*, the only one featuring love stories where Christian faith is the primary ingredient in a marriage relationship.

Sign up today to receive your first set of four, never before published Christian romances. Send no money now; you will receive a bill with the first shipment. You may cancel at any time without obligation, and if you aren't completely satisfied with any selection, you may return the books for an immediate refund!

Imagine. . .four new romances every four weeks—two historical, two contemporary—with men and women like you who long to meet the one God has chosen as the love of their lives. . .all for the low price of $9.97 postpaid.

To join, simply complete the coupon below and mail to the address provided. **Heartsong Presents** romances are rated G for another reason: They'll arrive *Godspeed!*